WHEN SHE'S BROKEN

BRIANN DANAE

Copyright © 2018 by BriAnn Danae

Published by **Beyond The Book Publications**
www.BriAnnDanae.net

All Rights Reserved

No part of this book may be reproduced in any form without written consent of the publisher, except brief quotations in review form.

This is a work of fiction. Any characters, places, objects, references or similarities to actual events, real people, living or dead, or to real locals are intended to give the novel a sense of reality. Any similarity in other names, characters, places, and incidents are entirely coincidental and are solely of the Author's imagination.

When She's Broken
────────────────────

Written by
BriAnn Danae

WARNING!

Although love is shown through the pages of this book, please be aware that this novel contains physical, sexual, and verbal abuse. This could be very triggering for victims of domestic violence. Read at your own risk.

Preface

Lying stiff as a board, Astryd tried calming her rapid heartbeat down. Her nerves were damn near getting the best of her, but she couldn't allow them to. Not now. With her back facing him, her eyes were trained on the door leading to their bathroom. It was slightly cracked and letting in a glimmer of light. Inhaling a deep breath, she gently peeled the thick comforter from her frame and slowly eased from underneath the damp sheet. A thin layer of perspiration had long ago coated her body because she was so nervous. So anxious to finally be doing this.

Swallowing the anxiety down her throat, Astryd placed one foot onto the hardwood floor, and her body immediately froze with fear when she heard him begin to shift in bed. *Had I moved too much?* She thought as her closed eyes pooled with tears. He came in drunk five hours ago, a little past midnight wanting sex. He always wanted sex even if she wasn't in the mood. A silent prayer was sent up to God. Astryd was begging him to let this "man" remain sleep. When a light snore escaped him and echoed through their bedroom, she sighed with relief before placing her other foot on the ground.

On shaky legs, she was finally on her feet. She gripped her cell phone tightly in her right hand so it wouldn't slip out. The palms of her hands were extremely sweaty. Her stomach churned as realization settled in. Clad in all her nakedness, Astryd carefully tiptoed to their bathroom being sure to avoid the spot on the wood floor that creaked loudly once stepped on. Sweat rolled down her back as she stepped inside. Too afraid to look back, not wanting to at this point, she rushed to their massive walk-in closet.

The bathroom echoed much too loudly for the phone call she was about to make. Leaving the closet door slightly ajar, Astryd scrambled on her knees to the furthest part of the closet, sat against the wall and pulled her knees to her chest. The plush carpet felt amazing against her naked frame, and honestly, if she could, she'd much rather sleep in the closet than lie in bed with him every night.

She stared at the entrance of the closet for over two minutes with her listening skills tuned in to any movement. When she didn't hear any was when she finally unlocked her phone. The brightness from the screen had been dimmed to the point you could hardly see a thing on it, but she had trained herself to see and read everything even in darkness. She had been in it for so long; Astryd grew accustomed to it.

The ten-digit number she committed to memory stared back at her on the keypad. Having typed it more times than she'd like to admit; Astryd was finally ready to use it. Her hands shook uncontrollably, and chills covered her arms as the air conditioner kicked on.

I must do this.

In her mind, this was the only other option if she wanted her situation to change. Her life to change, yet again. All the bullshit, hurt, lies, pain, the emotional and physical abuse he put her through had taken a toll on her. Not just her body, but her mind and soul. Her toxic relationship had drained her of the happiness she used to be filled with. The days of smiling because it was genuinely done were of the past.

Designer clothing draped over her head and shoulders as she tapped the green phone button to connect the call. The first ring rocked her core as she struggled to control her breathing. For months, she had been planning this, and now she didn't know if it were such a great idea. Before she could hang up and take what she assumed was the coward way out, the operator answered the phone.

"Hi, may I help you?"

Silence.

Astryd was stuck. She didn't know what words to even use after having rehearsed them in her head a thousand times.

"Hi. How can I help you?" the young woman spoke again.

"Hi," Astryd replied in her soft whisper tone.

"Hi, ma'am. How can I help you this morning?"

It was five in the morning. She was praying the young woman could help her. Anybody at this point. Astryd couldn't help herself.

"Is this… is this the women's shelter?"

"It's the hotline for shelters, yes. Are you seeking shelter?"

Preface

Astryd's eyelids closed tightly. Her throat ached from the pain she felt having to answer the question, but she knew it had to be answered. Tears stung her eyes as she nodded her head.

"Yes. He's... he's so different now," she said more to herself.

"Are you currently in danger?" the woman asked as she began to take notes.

Astryd's eyes looked up to the door. When she didn't see him standing there, she shook her head from side to side.

"No. Not right now. I don't think I'm really in danger... I just. I guess I wanted to know my options," she let out quickly and quietly.

As the woman began to ask her an array of questions pertaining to her life, Astryd couldn't believe some of the things she had endured over the years. Her mind was boggled at the idea of being in a domestic violence relationship. To her, she just thought maybe he had gotten a little jealous over the years and loved her differently.

I'm being crazy. This was a bad idea.

"Hi. Are you still there?" the operator asked.

Astryd closed her eyes and sighed. "Yes. But, I think I'll just call back later. I don't think I can leave him yet."

"Are you sure? If you're in any danger, you can always call the poli-"

"Who you on the phone with?"

Astryd's eyes flew open, and she flinched so hard at the sound of his deep voice, the phone fell from her hand. When their eyes connected, she blinked back tears. Whatever answer he was looking for, she was terrified of giving it. In a pair of boxers and nothing else, Alonzo stood at the closet door with his hands behind his back waiting for her to answer him. Astryd shook her head from side to side.

"No one?" he questioned.

She shook her head again.

His jaw ticked. Making slow, long strides over to her, his 6'3 frame towered over hers as he bent down to pick up her phone. The operator was still on the line, and she was silently praying for the timid young woman.

"Who the fuck is this?" he boomed, making Astryd scramble to scoot away from him. Grabbing her thigh, he squeezed it tightly forcing her to stay directly in front of him.

The operator stayed quiet. For confidentiality purposes, she couldn't disclose who she was or what she did. Especially not in this type of situation.

Astryd's life could be on the line. When she didn't answer, he chuckled.

"A'ight. You don't want to answer? Maybe she will," he grimaced, pulling a gun from behind him.

Astryd went to scream, but he stopped her.

"Nah. Don't make noise now. You trying to fucking leave me?" he hissed as the gun grazed Astryd's scalp.

Afraid to move her head, she spoke in a shaky breath terrified of the lie she was about to tell. "No."

"That's what I heard, though. You can't leave me now? Then, when? And, whoever this is was going to help you?" he gritted through clenched teeth, wanting to slap her across her beautiful face.

Again, she shook her head no as a tear rolled down her cheek.

"You love me?" he asked.

"Yes," she voiced.

"If you love me, why you trying to leave me then?"

"I'm not. I promise," she sniffled. "I love you."

"You hear that mufucka? She loves me. But, clearly, she must love you too if she's trying to leave me. I hope you know you just got her killed."

BOOM!

Hopping up from her sleep, Astryd placed a hand on the side of her head and closed her eyes. *Fuck, it was a dream.* Her body was soaked in sweat, and her heart was beating faster than it ever had in her life. Struggling to breathe, her body quaked as she began to cry. The warm body lying next to her lifted before pulling Astryd into its embrace.

"What's the matter?" he asked softly, wrapping his arms around her waist.

She shook her head trying to get back to reality. "It felt so real. This dream."

"But, it wasn't. It was probably just a nightmare," he reassured her, before kissing her temple. "Let me get you something to drink."

Astryd nodded in the dark. "Okay."

When he climbed from the bed, she pulled her knees to her chest and sat staring at the bathroom door that was slightly opened displaying a glimmer of light. The same light in her dream. Her eyes were full of curiosity and hope. She was hoping this was the last dream she ever had like that. But, more importantly, she was curious as to why she had it.

Should it have been me, first?

The question burned her up inside, and whatever answer she needed to ease her mind was never going to come. It was too late.

Chapter One

"Astryd," Alonzo called out from the bedroom door.

She was sleeping a little too peacefully, and her alarm had gone off ten minutes ago. Tucked away underneath their white duvet, Astryd stretched her arms above her head and rolled over. The sun was shining directly in her face, and she groaned with annoyance. Not because she had to wake up, but because she wished Alonzo had gotten the girls ready this morning. She had literally just laid down a few hours ago.

After arriving home from work, the house was a complete mess, and of course, they waited until she was home, so she could clean up. Tossing the cover from over her head, that was yanked back anyway, she flinched at how close Alonzo was standing over her.

"Weren't you just by the door?" she asked, with a yawn.

"Yeah. Get up. It's almost seven-thirty. You done let that alarm go off for ten fucking minutes. Ashlee's gotta be at the daycare in a few."

Alonzo stared down at her as she looked up at him and wiped the sleep from her eyes. "Did you get her dressed? And, where's Ashlynn?"

"In the living room watching cartoons and eating cereal," he grumbled. "How does a two-year-old be that hungry as soon as they wake up?"

Astryd shrugged as she climbed from the bed and glared at his back. She knew he hadn't answered her question about getting Ashlee dressed because he hadn't. Thankfully, she was at the age now where she could dress herself on mornings like this. Instead of starting an argument so early, she decided to hold her tongue.

"I don't know. You work today?"

"Nah." The sound of her sucking her teeth made Alonzo turn around. "What you doing all that for?"

"I didn't do anything."

Alonzo shook his head. "Come here."

Walking over to him in nothing but a pair of panties and a tank top on, he pulled Astryd into his embrace with ease. Her 5'5, 136-pound frame melted into his as Alonzo gripped her ass. Five years into their relationship with two daughters, and a group of family members who stayed in their ear, Astryd was waiting for the day a shift happened within her home. Everything with them had been so routine for the last few years, and she needed change immediately before she lost it.

"What I tell you about questioning me, huh? Do I question you?" Alonzo asked, and Astryd so badly wanted to yell out yes but shook her head no.

"No."

"Aight, then. I know you tired, but you better watch that shit. Give me a kiss."

Wrapping her arms around his waist, she kissed him with stank breath and all. Alonzo didn't give a fuck. Having been the only man Astryd has been intimate with since they got together, he was used to it by now. The two met while she was in school in 2012 but didn't start dating until 2013. Alonzo was twenty-four when they met and still pursued the twenty-year-old. When Astryd popped up pregnant with their first daughter, Ashlee, not even a year into them being together, she dropped out of college and moved back home. Three years later, she had her youngest daughter, Ashlynn, and hadn't gone back since.

Now, at twenty-six the life he promised her while she was away in school and even when she dropped out, was a far cry from her reality today. Alonzo would literally go from one extreme to the next in seconds. The slightest mistake, the tone of her voice, style of dress, and even taking too long to pee some days triggered his anger issues. To this day, Astryd didn't understand what she did to make him flip the switch on her and the love they shared. Every move from the time she opened her eyes in the morning, to when she closed them at night was made with caution.

With a tight grip on her face, he smacked her ass and lightly shoved her away. "Hurry up and get back. I got shit to do today."

"I have to be at work at nine," she mumbled.

Alonzo stopped dead in his tracks. Astryd's frame shivered at the thought of him giving her a brutal beat down before she had to drop the girls off. Squeezing her eyes shut, she scolded herself for even mentioning her job. Alonzo hated that she worked and made it known every day she went in.

"Did I ask you what fucking time you had to be

at work? See, that's your problem. Get the fuck out my face 'fore I beat your ass and make you quit that dumb ass job," he hissed.

Scrambling to the bathroom connected to their bedroom, Astryd did as she was told. Not bothering to close the door, knowing Alonzo hated for her to have her own privacy, she left it open while she released her full bladder. She'd been holding it for so long, she was surprised she didn't have a UTI by now. Alonzo did ornery shit like not letting her go to the restroom in the middle of the night because, in his mind, she was sneaking off to talk to another man. His insecurities got on Astryd's nerves the most.

Any man Astryd dated would be proud to claim her as his woman. Her beauty was unmatched. Exotic in looks, but far from the stuck-up type, Astryd was a sight for sore eyes. Long, black, luscious hair framed her copper colored, narrow oval shaped face and flowed down her back. Her pointy nose was courtesy of her father's white and Asian race. Thick full lips, wide hips on a slim frame that sat upon long legs, and only a blink of breasts, were courtesy of her African American mother.

Unaware of the beauty she held, Astryd allowed

Alonzo to diminish her spirit. Hearing him degrade her for so long after she had finally built the courage up and grown into who she was as a young lady, he came and snatched her confidence away. In the mirror, as she brushed her teeth, she ran a hand through her hair and winced from the sore spot in her scalp. It was evidence of the brutal hair pulling Alonzo found the pleasure in doing some nights as he dug her guts out. He was past heavy-handed, but the pain was pleasure to him.

After quickly getting dressed for work and making sure the girls were ready, Astryd slipped out of the room with her purse tossed over her shoulder and headed downstairs to the living room. The giggles of her two-year-old, Ashlynn, filled the air bringing a smile to her face. There wasn't anything she loved more than being a mother. Her little girls brought meaning and light to her life, especially when it got so dark sometimes.

"Mommy!" Ashlynn giggled, as Alonzo tickled her round belly.

When she went to pick her up, Alonzo shot her a mean mug. "Don't you see me holding her," he hissed as more of a statement rather than a question.

Astryd nodded her head before focusing her

attention on Ashlee. Her first born was the spitting image of her mother. Her long ponytail swayed side to side as she adjusted her backpack with a sleepy grin on her face.

"Good morning, ladybug," Astryd said, kissing her forehead.

"Morning, Mommy. I'm sleepy."

"I can tell. You ready to go?"

Ashlee nodded just as Ashlynn came and clung to her mother's leg. Scooping her youngest baby girl up, she turned to Alonzo who was sitting back on the couch in a pair of shorts scrolling through his phone. In that brief moment, Astryd actually found him good looking. She was so deep into the light skin men are in thing back when they met, she was somewhat blinded by the chocolate cutie with a ton of flaws who approached her. Alonzo's smooth dark skin, dark brown eyes, and clean-cut fade used to mesmerize Astryd. His walk used to make her weak in the knees, and his once inviting smile just made her cringe now. She didn't understand how something so handsome could be so ugly inside until she met him.

"You done staring?" Alonzo asked, looking up from his phone.

"Can I see my keys?"

He cocked his head to the side.

"Please?"

He nodded his head toward the front door of their three-bedroom townhome. "They on the hook by the door."

"Okay. I'll be right back. Say bye, girls."

"Bye, Daddy," the girls sang, unaware of the tension in the air.

With Ashlynn on her hip and Ashlee's hand in hers, Astryd made her way out of their home and to their 2015 Toyota Camry. It was a gift from her grandmother, her mom's mother, Lola. Strapping the girls in Astryd climbed inside and immediately got frustrated. Once again, there was hardly any gas in the tank, and she had to drive all the way across town damn near to drop the girls off, come back, and then head to work. Squeezing her eyes shut, she prayed she could make it to all three without stopping for gas. It wasn't an option with her having to be at work in an hour.

Making it across town in twenty minutes which was good for a Monday, Astryd pulled into Lola's driveway and kept the car running. Unstrapping Ashlynn, she waved at her sister as Ashlee leaned over to kiss her cheek.

"See you later, Ashy boo," Ashlee giggled.

Lola was standing outside waiting for her grandbaby. "What's the matter with you?" she asked as soon as they approached.

"Just a rough morning. I need to stop and get gas before I go back and pick Lonzo up and still drop Ashlee off at daycare," she sighed heavily, feeling the tears she tried keeping tucked away surface.

"I'll take her. You know it never hurts to ask when you need help," Lola said softly but meant every word.

Astryd sniffled. "You already do so much. I don't want to feel like a burden."

"Hush. Go get my other grandbaby and handle your business. Had you not been about shit like that cousin of yours, you know I wouldn't offer."

Chuckling, Astryd nodded her head and gave her a hug. "Thank you, Grammy. Today is my late day, so I won't get here until around six. Is that okay?"

"That's fine. I'm not doing much else. Plus, Ashlynn is a good child and potty trained. Go on now," she shooed.

Telling Ashlee to come on, Astryd kissed her girls and told them she'd see them later before hopping back in the car. Looking at the time, she thanked God she had enough time to stop and get gas. It was going on 8:15, which left her time to at least toss five or ten dollars in the tank, make the drive home and still be at work on time. It was wishful thinking though.

Pulling into her driveway at 8:47, she called Alonzo's cell prepared to tell him to come outside, but of course, he didn't answer. Huffing, Astryd climbed from the car and jogged up the steps. Entering their home, Alonzo was laid out right where he had been when she left damn near an hour ago. The game system was loud, and the potent weed smell from his blunt was even louder.

"Lonzo, it's almost nine o'clock. I can't be late," she said, trying to sound like she wasn't whining.

Looking her way, his eyes roamed her body before he focused back on the game. Astryd stood there like a child who had just asked her parents' permission to have company, and they ignored her. Alonzo was good for that but let her have ignored him; all hell would break loose. Watching the time tick by on the DVR monitor, Astryd turned on her heels to head back to the car.

"Did I say you could walk away?" Alonzo asked calmly.

Fear crept up her spine at the simple question.

She didn't turn around to answer him, and there was no need to. In the few seconds she used to suck in a breath, Alonzo was up on her from behind. Delivering a swift punch to the side of her stomach, Astryd dared not make a whimper. The more noise she made, the more blows he'd provide. As she tucked her lips to keep her cry hidden, she thought back to how it had gotten this bad. If there was something she had done to make him go from the once charming man she had fallen head first for, to the vicious, lazy, abuser of a man, Astryd wanted to know what she did wrong.

"I don't know why you think you're running shit, but you're not. Take your ass to the car, and you better walk straight too," he hissed, giving her a slight shove.

Swallowing hard, she took a small step forward and opened the door. Knowing he was probably watching her from the peephole once the door closed, she held her composure and walked like she hadn't just been punched in her ribs. Easing into the car, her entire frame trembled as she licked her dry lips. Crying wasn't an option. Alonzo would just make her skip work and beat her ass until he felt she had a reason to cry. Leaning her head back on the seat, she closed her eyes and said a silent prayer to the Man above.

"Lord, please save me from this hell I'm in," she whispered just as Alonzo came strolling out of the house.

Climbing in the car, he adjusted the seat and backed out of the driveway. They didn't pull up to Astryd's job until 9:13, making her late once again. This was not how she wanted to start her week off, but she had no choice.

"Fix yo fucking face and give me a kiss before you walk in there," he spat before she could climb out.

Turning in her seat, she leaned over and pecked his lips with her eyes open. When she felt him smirk, she sighed and backed away. He wasn't smirking at the feel of her soft lips though. One of Astryd's coworkers was walking by and caught the two lip-locking. Being the asshole he was, Alonzo shot the girl a wink while Astryd wasn't looking. When Astryd's eyes landed on her strutting past the front of their car, it took everything in her not to say something to him. That'd just warrant her in a deal of trouble later on.

"Have a good day. I get off at 5:30," she told him opening her door.

"Aight. I love you A."

With her back to him, Astryd mumbled, "I love you too," before climbing out and closing the door.

The words left a bitter taste on her tongue every time she was forced to speak them. If what he was giving her was supposed to feel like love, she'd never want to know what hate felt like.

Chapter Two

The work week had flown by, and Astryd couldn't complain. Well, she could, but she was grateful to even still have a job. One that paid well at that. Working at an assisted living facility hadn't been her dream job, in fact, it wasn't the first option when she began her hunt for work. When she went in for the interview, she knew she didn't meet all the qualities they were searching for in an employee but gave her the position anyway. Her kind spirit and willingness to learn is what sealed the deal for her employer.

Staring down at her phone screen as it rang, she sucked her teeth when the call went to voicemail for the third time. Alonzo was supposed to have picked her up over thirty minutes ago, and yet he hadn't returned a single phone call or showed his face.

"He knows I get off at one on Fridays," she grumbled, feeling annoyed as hell.

Popping a squat on the bench, Astryd enjoyed the cool August breeze as she dialed up her best friend, Honey, for a ride. It wouldn't be the first time nor the last. She just prayed she wasn't busy. After the second ring, Honey answered in her angelic tone making Astryd smile.

"Hey boo!"

"Honey, love," Astryd cooed. "Hey. Are you busy?"

"Nope. About to go get some food with Greigh and Lee, what's up?"

Her eyes closed, and face bunched up. Asking for favors was extremely hard for Astryd. Even after over a decade of friendship, she still felt a way about it.

"Can you get me from work, please," she hurriedly let out, then held her breath.

"Girl, yeah. I'm like five minutes from there. You hungry?"

Astryd released a deep breath and smiled. "Yeah. I could eat."

"Bet. I'm on the way boo."

"Okay. I'm outside. Thank you so much. I'll give you gas mon—"

"Byyye. I ain't trying to hear that," Honey fussed with a light laugh before hanging up in her best friend's face.

Gas money wasn't going to change the fact that they had solid years of friendship under their belt. Back in high school if Astryd slid her a five or ten for gas it was cool, 'cause Honey was the only one with a car, but now they were grown. She did for Astryd because she loved her, not because she wanted something in return. That included gas money.

When Honey pulled up in her coke white Benz with the peanut butter seats, Astryd stood to her feet and met her at the curb. Climbing in, she exhaled as the soft seats seemed to massage her tense body.

"Hey girl," Honey said smiling. "How was work?"

"Strange for a Friday, but I'm used to it," she chuckled. "Where you coming from?"

"The shop. I had a last-minute client walk in, right before we decided to go out to eat."

Honey and Greigh both used to work at the same nail shop but now owned their own shop. Their clientele was through the roof and hardly did they ever have time to take walk-in's, but Friday's until 12:30 Honey took them. She'd extend her hours on some Friday's, but today she needed a lunch break. Her stomach was touching her damn back.

"I see you dyed your hair again," Astryd noticed, giving her friend an appreciative look.

Honey was the prettiest girl you'd lay eyes upon with her bright skin decorated in light brown freckles, crimson red hair and penny colored eyes, she most definitely stood out in any crowd.

"Yes. I don't know why I can't shake this red. I love it," she replied, hopping on the highway.

"So does Jamir," Astryd said, speaking of Honey's man.

"Girl yes. He calls me his little hood rat superstar," she laughed shaking her head.

"You'd look good with black. You should try it."

Honey smirked and looked over at her. "I think I will. What's been up with you? I feel like I haven't seen you in forever. I know I be busy with work and traveling, but that's no excuse."

"No, it's okay. We all have lives. I've been good, though. Working, taking care of the girls and enjoying watching them grow. I swear Ashlee is too much for me sometimes," she snickered.

"I'm sure she acts just like you. Sweet as hell, but baby don't let that attitude surface."

"Oh, whatever. My attitude is nonexistent now."

"Mhm. As if that nigga Alonzo don't be pissing you off."

Astryd shrugged. Alonzo did way more than piss her off. He was the reason she was sitting passenger side of a vehicle that wasn't hers.

"Not really. He's getting better," she said softly, not wanting to give any indication that he was beating her ass for breakfast, lunch, dinner, and a midnight snack.

Honey just nodded as she cruised down Lindbergh. St. Louis was their hometown, and neither of them ever wanted to leave it back in the day but getting a new address in a different state was starting to look more and more appealing by the day. Honey for business purposes, and Astryd for an array of reasons. The main one being her safety. Every day she was gambling with her life by staying with Alonzo, but she couldn't see leaving him for anyone or thing better. Not yet at least.

Sitting in the booth at 54th Street Bar & Grill, Astryd sipped on her water as her eyes kept dropping to her phone. It was sitting on the table and had been since they arrived. Alonzo hadn't called back yet, but she knew he would and didn't want to miss his phone call.

"I know that waitress better stop looking over here like she knows us," Greigh fussed with a frown on her face.

"Y'all are known for doing nails, G. Relax tough ass," Lee snickered.

"Nah. She looks like she has an attitude for real. I don't like that. Anyway, before she makes me get out of character in here... what's been going on?"

The four had been close for a while now. Lee and Greigh were best friends, and Honey was Lee's cousin. Their bond grew even closer after a freak accident that involved Lee being in a coma for almost a month.

Astryd sat back and listened to Lee speak on her and her husband, Demir's, married life now. The glow radiating from her skin was just as bright as the one from her wedding ring. Love looked good on Lee, and after all she had been through she deserved every ounce her man gave.

Though it shouldn't have, a wave of envy came over Astryd. Not because she was jealous of any of the women in her presence, but because she was just content with being Alonzo's baby mama. As her girls spoke so highly of their partners and the moves they were making to secure them a lifestyle of wealth, Astryd found herself struggling to answer the question regarding what Alonzo was doing for work. He wasn't working; it was as simple as that.

"He um… well, he's in between jobs right now," she answered.

"In between? Girl, if he's looking for work, *Indeed* has plenty of job openings, okay?" Greigh laughed but was serious.

"Seriously friend," Honey agreed. "Lots of people are hiring right now."

"I'll let him know," she replied sipping from her straw.

They continued chatting until their food was brought out. Having not eaten all day, Astryd tore into her tequila wrappers, waffle fries, and gringo dip. She was so focused on her plate, she didn't take a breather or look up until a girl walked up to their table.

"Hey, Honey. I thought that was you," the girl chirped.

"Hey, girl. What's up?"

"Nothing much," she said giving the table a wave of her hand. "I heard your cousin is getting out soon. You excited?"

Honey chuckled at the audacity of her question.

"Yeah, you? Heard you been ducked off while he been away."

She waved her hand dismissively. "Oh, don't listen to him. I've been right where he left me. I'll be seeing you around though. Maybe we can link up once he gets out."

"Eh, I doubt it, but have a good day girl," Honey replied making the girls chuckle.

When the girl walked away, Lee was the first one to speak up. "Was that Baylei?"

Honey nodded. "Mhm. That was her hoe ass. She gone bring up my cousin like he really fucks with her."

"He's getting out soon?" Astryd asked, unable to hold the question in any longer.

"Yep. Should be touching down next week if I'm not mistaken. Your brother didn't let you know about the welcome home party?"

Astryd shook her head no as a feeling she hadn't felt in years took over her body. She couldn't quite describe what it was, but she no longer had an appetite. "No, I haven't talked to him in like a week."

"Oh. Well, yeah. We're throwing him a welcome home party next weekend. Y'all should come through," Honey suggested.

"Bitch, is that how you invite someone out?" Greigh joked.

"It sure is, and you and Esmin better be there. Tell that nigga to bring some wings, too," Honey laughed.

"Nah. Nope. You aren't about to use my man for his business. Is your cousin still fine?" Greigh asked in a whisper like Esmin would pop up from another table and scold her ass for speaking that way about another man.

Pursing her lips together, Honey nodded with a smirk. "Yep. And he got buff as hell. But don't even worry about him. You got a man."

"Shiiiit. Ain't nothing wrong with looking," Greigh laughed, and Lee shook her head in amusement.

While they laughed and giggled, Astryd was thinking of a way she could convince Alonzo to not attend the welcome home party with her. She wanted no distractions when her eyes landed upon him. The him who could have been her man instead of Alonzo. Memories of them and what they could have been flooded her brain, but not for long.

The vibration of her phone against the wooden table made her flinch so hard, the ladies all looked at her like something was wrong. Astryd gave them a soft smile, before answering Alonzo's call and turning her volume down.

"Where the fuck you at?" he asked calmly.

It was damn near two hours later, and that's what he wanted to know? Not give an apology for leaving her stranded or ask how work was? His only concern was why she wasn't at the home they shared. Astryd was damn near spooked to answer his question but knew he wouldn't let her off the phone without answering.

"I'm out to eat with Honey. She picked me up from work," she said lowly.

"Who else I hear talking?" he hissed.

Astryd swallowed hard. Their waiter, a male, had just walked back over and was asking how everything tasted. He stood around a little too long trying to make sure he earned his tip.

"That was the waiter, bae."

The line went quiet for a full minute before Alonzo said anything. "Aight. The girls with my mama for the weekend."

"Okay. Do you want me to bring you some food home?" she asked sweetly.

"Nah. Just hurry your ass home to me so we can spend some time together."

His reply made Astryd smile. It'd been so long since they spent quality time with one another, she almost asked if he could come and get her but knew that'd be just enough reason for him to come inside and show his ass.

"I'll be home soon. Love you."

"Yeah. You better."

The line disconnected and Astryd sat there with a goofy grin on her face. The appetite she lost before her call was back. Dipping her fry into the dip, she chewed slowly as they all stared at her with smirks on their faces.

"What?" she questioned.

"That was that, 'Bring your ass home so I can drop this dick in your belly,' phone call, huh?" Greigh laughed. "I know that smile all too well."

Astryd rolled her eyes playfully. "I bet you do."

An hour later with full bellies, the group of ladies hugged before parting ways. Astryd and Honey headed to her car, so she could drop her off at home. Seeing the time on the dashboard made Astryd sigh heavily. Though Alonzo was calm when he called, in the back of her mind, Astryd knew her going out with her girls without consulting with him first would most likely lead to an argument. An argument she was not in the mood to have.

Alonzo had out of nowhere over the years become constantly jealous. It was so bad, she'd hate to even be around his friends. One wrong reply or saying to them, and Alonzo's mind immediately went to her having some kind of ties to them sexually. Controlling her daily activities was another favorite of his. Knowing Astryd's favorite thing to do to pass time was play games on her phone, he'd keep it from her for hours on end only to ignore her. Him being unemployed was the worst though, especially on her off days. It drove Astryd crazy.

"You good over there?" Honey asked as they pulled onto her street.

Swallowing down her nervousness, Astryd gave her friend a smile. "Yes. Just tired is all. I'm glad the girls are gone for the weekend. I can possibly try to sleep in," she giggled.

"I know that's right. I can't wait until Jamir, and I have one of our own."

"You guys planning?" Astryd asked.

Her first, Ashlee, was not planned at all. She blindsided the young couple but was a blessing nonetheless.

"It'd be nice too, but we'll see. I'm in a really good space mentally and financially, we both are, but Jamir wants to be married first."

Astryd grinned widely. "Oh shoot. Look at him." They shared a chuckle as she pulled into the driveway next to her parked car.

"Right, girl. That's my baby. So, if he wants to wait until marriage, I am perfectly fine with that."

The smile on Honey's face made Astryd's cheeks rise. She was elated for her girl. Jamir was such a gentleman whenever she was in his presence. He'd be the perfect husband; something Astryd thought Alonzo would be, but she wasn't so sure anymore. Before she let her negative thoughts ruin their moment, she cleared her throat and shook her head.

"I'm happy for you. Let me get in here and spend some time with my man. Maybe I'll get a ring too, hell."

As they embraced in a hug, Honey grabbed her wrist when they broke away. Astryd gave her a questioning gaze.

"Any man would be lucky as hell to give you his last name," Honey told her, with a soft, reassuring smile.

"Thank you boo. I'll call you later and thank you for swooping me up."

"Of course. I'll text you when I make it home."

Climbing from the car, Astryd took slow,

measured breaths to calm her racing heartbeat down. With each step she made to the door, her stomach flip-flopped. Using her key, she walked inside, and to her surprise, it was silent. The lamp by the couch was on, but there was no sign of Alonzo. Heading upstairs to their room, Astryd's confirmation of him being in bed was right. Sprawled out in their bed with his chest lightly rising and falling, Astryd stared at the man she used to love with resentment in her heart.

I hate him, she said in her head. It was the truth. She was always told that hate was such a mean word, but that's the only one she could muster up to describe her feelings toward him. Her eyes darting to her pillow beside him and the thought to smother his ass in his sleep crossed her mind. As quickly as it'd come, it left. The only reason she didn't inch her way toward him was because of her girls. Killing him would break their hearts. Sighing in frustration because she couldn't escape him, Astryd turned on her heels and headed to the bathroom.

Turning on the shower, she began stripping from her clothing. As the mirror began to fog, Astryd hummed a light melody her mother used to sing to her as a little girl. She couldn't quite remember all the words, but the few she did know soothed her. With her eyes closed, her mind drifted to a time in her life where things were much simpler. Life wasn't so complicated in figuring out and had it been, her mother assisted her in doing so.

"I miss you so much," she said in a throaty tone as a tear slid down her cheek.

"Why you miss me? I'm right here?"

The sound of Alonzo so close to her made Astryd flinch hard as hell, and her eyes popped open wide. She didn't know when he had walked in or how long he had been standing there, but the look on his face was not a pleased one. Swallowing hard, Astryd stared back at him in the almost completely fogged mirror. Inching closer to her, Alonzo grabbed the back of her neck, and she tensed up. When he began to caress it, she relaxed some.

"Who you miss?" he asked lowly, pressing his pelvis into her ass.

"M-My Mom."

His grip tightened. "You lying to me?"

"No. I swear."

"If I didn't know any better, I'd think you were

talking about that man you went out to dinner with."

Astryd's face frowned up. "I wasn't...I didn't go out to eat with another man. I went with Honey, Lee, and Greigh."

"Yeah? So, where the leftovers at? You ain't bring me no food home?"

"Y-You told me you didn't want anything," Astryd let out as chill bumps coated every inch of her body.

The mirror had now been completed covered, and she couldn't see him, which was probably a good thing. His jaw clenched before his hand came up to her head and yanked a handful of her hair. Astryd's head snapped back so roughly, he could have broken her neck.

"Did I say that or the nigga you was with tell you not to bring me anything home?" he asked calmly.

Astryd's mind ran wild trying to muster up the correct answer. Evidently, she hadn't thought quickly enough. Squeezing her jaw tightly, Alonzo forced her to open up her mouth and roughly shoved his fingers down her throat. Immediately, Astryd gagged at the forceful move.

"If I have to go to bed hungry, so do you. You

better throw all that shit up, and I mean it," he hissed evilly, before yanking her to the toilet.

"L-Lonzo, please," she cried, but it fell upon deaf ears.

Holding her head back, he forced his fingers down her throat once more, and the food Astryd devoured earlier, came rushing out of her mouth and into the toilet bowl. Tears clouded her vision as the pull on her hair intensified.

"Bitch, you think I'm stupid?" Alonzo growled, slapping her upside the head. "You think you gon' leave me for another nigga?"

Before she could answer, his fingers were ramming the back of her throat and more vomit emitted from her. Tears rolled down her cheeks the more she threw up. Alonzo had beat her plenty times before, but this was a new low. One Astryd couldn't believe he had gone to. After shoving his fingers down her throat until she was dry heaving and dehydrated, Alonzo stood at the sink and washed his hands.

"You better have your ass showered and, in this bed before I finish smoking this blunt," he told her.

Astryd couldn't even nod her head. She was so weak, and throat was so sore, she was sure he had torn her esophagus. It pained her to swallow. She wished he'd just walk away so she could let her tears fall in peace – or what she considered it to be. The swift kick to her side made Astryd groan lowly.

"You heard what the fuck I said. Have your ass in this fucking bed," he spat.

"O-Okay,' she replied barely audible.

When she heard him walk away, she listened for that sound in the floor to let her know he was enough distance away before releasing her breath. Having the door closed and letting her pain out without him hearing wasn't going to happen. On trembling legs, Astryd struggled to inhale a deep breath. Once she was to her feet, she didn't bother going to the mirror, she just climbed in the shower. The scolding hot water stung against her body, but she'd take that pour down of a beating any day over the ones Alonzo handed out.

Squeezing her eyes shut tightly, Astryd didn't cry. She just thanked God her girls weren't present to accidentally walk in or hear their altercation. She'd never forgive herself if they had.

Chapter Three

Rushing around her mess of a room, Astryd hopped on one leg while putting her shoe on. Honey was a few minutes away from her house, and she still hadn't done a thing to her hair. When her phone rang, she began to panic. Time was apparently not on her side. Snatching it up from the bed, she answered quickly.

"I'm almost ready," she said, walking into the bathroom.

"Good, because I'm pulling into the driveway," Honey replied.

"Geez! What'd you do? Fly your ass here?"

Honey laughed. "You know my aunt doesn't live that far away. Just hurry your narrow behind up before he gets there."

"Okay, okay. Give me two minutes, tops."

Honey mumbled an 'mhm' and hung up. Tossing her phone on the counter, Astryd hurriedly brushed through her hair before running the flat iron through it a few times. As thick and long as it was, she was glad it decided to play nice today. After adding a little mascara, a light coat of nude gloss, thin gold necklace and a squirt of her favorite perfume, she released a huff.

"Shit, I forgot how much energy it takes to get fine," she let out.

She didn't have time to give herself a once over. Rushing back inside the room, she grabbed her purse and headed outside. After locking the door, she walked over to Honey's passenger side and climbed in.

"Sorry. Was that long?" she asked, trying to catch her breath.

When Honey didn't reply, Astryd faced her. "What? What's wrong?"

"Giiirl. Two kids where?!" Honey yelped, in sheer excitement.

Bashfully, Astryd waved her off. "Stop."

"I'm serious A! You look good, girl. Damn. I wish I were those jeans," she joked, making Astryd crack a smile.

"I've gained some weight, so they're a little tight. Dang. Should I change? I mean, I look okay, right?" she asked, nervously while pulling the visor down to check herself out.

"You look fine as hell. Whatever you been eating, let me know, okay? My ass can't gain two pounds, and if I do, I swear the shit goes to my forehead."

The friends cracked up laughing as she pulled off down the street.

"Your job let you off work? I can't believe it," Astryd said getting comfortable for the fifteen-minute car ride to Honey's Aunt Deb's house.

"Yes. I let my supervisor know months in advance that I'd need this day off. Had she not given it, my ass was calling in," she said seriously.

"I know he's happy to be home."

"He is. He tried playing it off when I last talked to him, but I could hear the excitement in his voice. I hate the damn justice system, I swear," she fussed as Astryd sat in deep thought.

She felt the same way, but for a different reason.

"Same, girl."

"Your car was in the driveway. Is something wrong with it?"

Astryd shook her head and told her the lie she

had rehearsed before she arrived. Well, the lie she was told.

"No. Alonzo went out of town and accidentally took my keys with him," she replied with a roll of her eyes.

"How'd he do that? He does know you have the girls, right?"

She nodded. "I don't know, girl. And he knows. They're with my cousin until tonight, so it's fine."

The truth was, Alonzo took her keys, so she couldn't go anywhere. That wasn't stopping Astryd though. She wouldn't miss this welcome home party.

"That's what's up. Is Winston going to be here? I haven't seen him in so long."

"No. He couldn't make it down. The season is underway, but he promised to be here for Ashlee's birthday at the end of October."

Winston is Astryd's older brother by two years, at age twenty-eight. He was away being an assistant football coach for the defensive line at Missouri State University. With this being his first year apart of the program, missing a game, especially a home game, wasn't a good look. He sent his brotherly love through Astryd, and when he could welcome home his boy the correct way he would.

"She does have a birthday coming up. You made plans yet?" Honey asked as they pulled onto her aunt's packed street. She just knew someone had stolen her parking spot.

"Not yet. You know Ashlee's a diva, so we'll see what she decides on this year," Astryd chuckled.

Letting her eyes do a sweep of the block aligned with vehicles, her heart swelled at the love D'Haven was being shown. He had been locked down for far too many years in the family's eyes, but they were glad he was finally home. Once Honey found a parking spot in the neighbor's driveway, they climbed out and headed toward her aunt's house. Loud music and laughter filled the air as they walked through the front door.

"Why your ass ain't go through the back like everybody else!" Deb, D'Haven's mama, hollered at her niece.

"I'm not everybody else, duh," Honey laughed. "Plus, I have someone with me I thought you'd like to see."

Stepping through the kitchen walkway, Astryd gave Deb a soft smile. "Hey, Ms. Deb."

"Girl! Don't hey me. Your ass better give me a hug. I ain't saw you in how long?" she fussed, walking over to Astryd, pulling her into a hug.

The embrace of the short, fluffy, full of life woman made Astryd smile. She couldn't remember the last time she saw Deb, but it had definitely been a while. When they released one another, Deb gave her a big grin.

"Still pretty as I remember. How them babies of yours doing?"

"They're fine. Getting big," Astryd replied just as someone from the family rushed in from the back door.

"He's pulling up!" the young boy yelled out.

Quickly, Deb dried her hands and clapped. "Let's head outside to greet my baby."

"He's a grown man auntie," Honey joked, and Deb swatted her arm.

"Shut yo ass up. That's my baby for as long as I live."

The backyard was packed to capacity. Astryd had a large family, but hers didn't have shit on the size of Honey's. This wasn't even all of them; just the ones Deb saw fit to be in attendance when D'Haven touched down. To those who didn't as much as ask about him, they were not welcome on her property. She didn't give a fuck about them being blood or not.

Licking her lips, Astryd told herself to relax.

She kept fidgeting with the bracelet on her wrist, tucking her hair behind her ear, and chewing on the corner of her lip. She was a nervous wreck and didn't know why. Well, she knew why, but would never admit it out loud. Seeing her first real crush, who she was forced to get over, for the first time in years had her losing her cool. Seeing everyone with their phones out as D'Haven made his way toward the backyard, Astryd was desperately searching for the breath she needed to inhale at the sight of him.

Goddamn. She thought she said in her head, but when someone next to her chuckled, her eyes bucked.

"Yeah, my brother is still fine, ain't he?" Demi, D'Haven's twenty-one-year-old sister said, grinning.

Not bothering to give her a response, she just cleared her throat and focused on the sight before her. And, damn was he a sight to see. He looked better than Astryd could remember, but then again, it had been years since then. If her lips weren't pressed tightly together, she was sure she'd have drool seeping from the corner of her mouth, decorating her shirt.

"Welcome home!" the group of friends and family cheered once he was closer to them.

When D'Haven hit them with a smile, Astryd

about fell out. It was gorgeous. He had the type of smile that made you smile on the inside and out. It was breathtaking and had snatched the little air Astryd had managed to inhale right away. She licked her lips and adjusted her stance as she took all of him in, and damn was there a lot.

D'Haven's milk chocolate body looked as if all he did while away was pump iron, and for the most part, he had. The bulge in his arms and tight fit of the plain white V-neck he was wearing should've been a sin the way it clung to his body. Honey wasn't lying when she said he had gotten buff. His athletic physique was mouthwatering; goddamn drool worthy. His height made Astryd want to see how long it took to climb him. The closer he got, Astryd realized how much better looking he was up close.

The haircut he got before popping up to his mom's crib was worth it. Astryd wanted to thank his barber twice for such a job well done. His thick, black hair was cut low showing off his small curls and perfect line-up. Astryd was thankful he had a goatee and thin mustache rather than a beard because his chiseled jawline made her lower parts pulsate every time his juicy lips moved. The structure of his face, in general, was so masculine.

So sexy. So... everything Astryd didn't know she was missing out on until now. D'Haven Graham was all man, that was for sure. If his physical features didn't let that be known, the depth of his voice did.

"Ladies, y'all missed me?" He asked jokingly, with a handsome grin.

The question rolled off his tongue so smoothly, Astryd didn't realize he was even in her presence because she was so far gone. Blinking her eyes and clearing her throat, she wrung her hands together to keep from reaching out and touching him. As he hugged Honey, his eyes were on Astryd. They were piercing through her soul and giving her shivers.

"I'm so happy you're home!" Honey beamed smiling widely.

"Yes! Me too. I missed your big head so much," Demi chimed in.

"I missed y'all too, but y'all already know that. Astryd, how you doing?" he asked coolly, waiting for her to embrace him in a hug but she couldn't.

Hell, she couldn't move let alone speak to the man. When Honey bumped her arm, she jumped a little and stuck her hand out.

"H-Hey. Welcome home. You look good," she said before she could catch herself. Her stomach dropped when he hit her with that panty-wetting smile.

"You look good too," he replied, letting his eyes do a slow, torturous sweep over her frame.

Under his torturous gaze, Astryd's body trembled. The high-waisted jeans she had on outlined her childbearing hips, and small but plump ass. She didn't have much up top to look at in the white one-piece she was rocking, but that was fine with D'Haven. Her nipples were harder than the stare down he was giving her. After being locked up for five years, he drank her beauty in with the utmost appreciation.

"Girl. What you trying to give him a handshake for? You better hug my cousin," Honey said, nudging her D'Haven's way. She practically fell into his embrace, but he caught her.

Quickly, she wrapped her arms around his bulky frame and stepped back. The smell and feel of him had her hyperventilating. He was perfection in Astryd's eyes and as lonely as she had been feeling, that wasn't a good thing. D'Haven wanted to hold on to her a little longer, but he knew she wasn't going to let him. Not now at least.

"Come on, brother. Let's go mingle," Demi said, ending their silent staring contest.

He gave Astryd and Honey another grin before allowing his sister to pull him in the direction of her friends. Some friends who were eye-fucking D'Haven like crazy. When Honey looked around, it seemed the women who weren't family all were. Astryd was stuck again. His intoxicating cologne was lingering in the air, and she wanted to bottle the shit up for her own personal use.

"Girl look at these grown ass women lusting over my cousin," Honey scoffed.

"Do you not see how fine he is? Shit! I'm ready to see what that cheating life is about," Greigh said, walking up on them. They had walked in right when D'Haven was walking away.

"And be all hurt when Esmin leaves your ass," Honey laughed but stopped when she saw the look on Astryd's face.

"A, what's wrong?"

Shaking her head from the life she imagined having with D'Haven, Astryd looked towards her girls. "Nothing. Was just in deep thought."

"You thinking about cheating too, A? I won't tell your nigga if you don't tell mine," Greigh said playfully and her eyes bucked when she felt someone lightly smack her booty.

"Thought I was Esmin, huh?" Lee laughed.

"She sure did. You should've seen the look on her face," Honey laughed.

"I don't know why she's talking about cheating when she knows what happened the last time she was even texting a guy."

Greigh rolled her eyes at Lee. "Malone was nice. Real nice. If Es wouldn't have gotten his shit together, I sure was going to fool around with him."

"I'm good on that. I was just... you know... admiring, I guess," Astryd answered, and they all snickered.

"Yeah, girl. We know. Let's go get some food. I'm hungrier than a kid who just came home from school," Greigh said.

"Kids be starving like they ain't ate all day," Honey added as they laughed and walked across the yard to where the long tables were filled with trays of food in warmers.

Following behind then, Astryd's eyes fell on the girl who had walked over to their table while they were out to eat last week. She couldn't help but notice the way the girl was touching all over D'Haven and smiling in his face.

"Is that his girlfriend or something?" she found herself asking Honey in a whisper.

Lifting her head after piling macaroni on her

plate, Honey sucked her teeth. "Girl, nah. That's his ex, Baylei. I don't know who invited her, but I'm sure it was Demi's doing. The bitch ain't been coming around, so I don't know why she thinks she's about to be now."

The disdain in Honey's tone let it be known that Baylei wasn't her favorite person, but she couldn't say the same for D'Haven. While she tried not to stare, it was hard. D'Haven was the man of the hour and he silently, even feet away, commanded her attention. When he looked up from talking to Baylei, his eyes landed on Astryd's who was staring back at him. Shooting her a wink and playful grin made her hastily turn away, breaking their connection.

D'Haven chuckled before walking away from whatever Baylei was trying to convince him into doing. If there was one thing that stuck with him while in jail, it was to never let another muthafucka convince him of doing something he knew he had no business doing. One time was all it took for D'Haven to learn his lesson, and what Baylei was trying to be on in broad daylight wasn't a go for him.

"Wait," she called out after him. "I wasn't done talking."

"I was though. You got a lot to say for someone who I haven't heard from since I went in," he chuckled not hurt at all by her actions. "You enjoy yourself without my presence."

"Don't act like that," Baylei cooed. "I promise it wasn't intentional, D. Can we start over?" She asked softly, grabbing ahold of his arm.

Watching her plump lips move as she ran a tongue over them, D'Haven's dick twitched. Baylei was the last girl to have given him head before he was locked up. In fact, she was the last piece of ass as well, but it had been years, and D'Haven wasn't pressed at all for pussy. Not from her at least. He was backed up like crazy and though her trying to top him off right now in the whip or the bathroom of his mama's house couldn't go down, he'd gladly take her up on her offer later in the evening, though.

"I'll come find you when I'm about to leave," he told her.

Smiling wide, Baylei nodded her head. "Okay."

Watching her walk away with a little more pep in her step, D'Haven shook his head before heading to catch up on lost time with his folks. It had been way too long since he had seen them. Many had kept in touch, the ones who really fucked with him, and some… well, they weren't in attendance. Deb wasn't playing when it came to her son's welcome home party and well-being. Walking up on his group of male cousins and closest homeboys, they slapped hands while his righthand man Tech tried handing him a blunt.

Chuckling, D'Haven waved him off. "I'm good. They got me meeting with my PO first thing in the morning."

"Damn. They serious ain't they," Tech said, inhaling the potent weed.

"Yeah, but I ain't worried. I'm just trying to knock this shit out and move on with my life."

They all nodded in agreement. Plenty of them were or had been on papers. The time it took to adjust back into society after being locked up was tough. D'Haven wasn't trying to jeopardize his freedom in any way. The only thing on his mind right now was kicking it with his family.

"I see you eyeing your girl," Tech smirked.

D'Haven's eyes were glued to Astryd and how fine she was even from a distance. He couldn't keep his eyes off her. She had surely matured over the years.

"That ain't mine. Not yet. She still with her baby daddy?"

"Yeah, last I heard she was. Got two pretty little girls. They don't ever come around for real. I'm surprised she even here without that nigga," Tech offered.

D'Haven just ran a hand over his head as he watched her walk into the house through the back door. Before his mind could register what was going on, his feet were moving, following behind her. Chuckling, Tech shook his head just as Baylei walked up on them with a frown on her face.

"I know he going after her," she spat.

"What that got to do with you?"

Baylei rolled her eyes. "I don't see what's so special about her. That nigga keeps blowing me off and I'ma let you take his spot."

Tech laughed out loud. "Say, man. Get yo ass out my face. Ain't no spot. You a hoe."

Blowing the smoke from his mouth, his eyes roamed her frame freely. He had seen her naked a handful of times, and though she had a nice body, Baylei was ran through. After D'Haven got locked up, she held him down for a little while but was nowhere in sight for the remainder of his sentence. She was somewhere getting fucked by one of his niggas and doing her. Tech wasn't the first one, and probably wouldn't be the last. When he told

D'Haven what was up, he didn't even trip. Not for long anyway. He knew what type of broad Baylei was from the jump, but never thought she'd fuck his niggas. That was on her though.

"I wasn't a hoe when I was sucking your dick the other night," she hissed, as a few of his boys chuckled.

"Nah. You were one then too. Go sack chase another nigga, ma. I ain't it."

"Fuck you, Tech! I should tell your baby mama about your dog ass!"

"What's that gon' solve?" he asked, laughing. "She gon' beat yo ass and be right back home with our child. Get yo ass on fore' I have one of D'Haven's cousins dog your ass for real."

Sucking her teeth hard, Baylei shoved him in his arm before stomping off to find where D'Haven ventured off to. She couldn't believe the way Tech was acting with her, but she should've known he wasn't about to wife her ass. The first opportunity she saw to hop on his dick with D'Haven not around, she did. The only reason D'Haven didn't care was because he never loved her. Yeah, he had feelings for her, but his time in jail made him realize she was just convenient, and he was young; 23 at the time. It was five years later, and she was not the woman he planned to settle down with ever.

Stopped by Demi on her way inside the house, Baylei ran down what had just transpired. Inside the house, D'Haven was smiling at Astryd from behind as she swayed to the beat of the music while pouring herself a drink. There were drinks outside in the cooler, but she needed something slightly stronger. Sipping the sweet red wine from the glass, her taste buds danced with excitement.

"It must be good," D'Haven said, making her jump and grab her chest as the wine traveled down the wrong pipe.

Violent coughs escaped her mouth as she turned to face him. When she got her breathing under control, she cleared her throat. "Jesus, D'Haven. Don't walk up on me like that."

The frightened look in her eyes made the grin on his face drop. "My fault. I didn't mean no harm."

She took a deep breath. "It's fine."

When he stepped closer, Astryd swallowed hard. Being this close to him again was torturous. As he towered over her, she did everything in her power not to look him in his eyes. Those gentle eyes that she was sure would suck out every dark secret she was trying to keep contained. So, instead, she focused on his arms. They were big, but not scary big. The few tattoos decorating them told some stories unknown to her, and others she knew well.

"I make you nervous still?" he asked.

Astryd's neck grew warm. "N-No. Why would you think that?"

"You can't even look at me in the face. I hope you don't think I'm mad about what happened."

"You should be. It was my fau—"

D'Haven hushed her next words. Him going to jail had nothing to do with her. Not in the way she had made up in her mind. While he was locked up, Winston had visited and let him know that she was so hurt how the entire situation had played out. He wanted to reach out to her, and he did a few times, but Alonzo shut that down quick. Wasn't no nigga behind bars or not going to be calling her phone. Neither of them was given a chance to express their feelings about the situation, and today wouldn't be that day.

"No, it wasn't. Don't ever say that again," he said, forcing her to look him in the face.

The slight touch of his index knuckle lifting her head made flutters swarm through Astryd's belly. Staring in his eyes, she blinked slowly and smiled softly. D'Haven saw the forced smile on her face, but it never reached her eyes. That didn't sit right with him, and he didn't know why. He hadn't seen this girl in years, yet he was drawn to her so magnetically, he couldn't pull away if he tried. Tucking her hair behind her ear, Astryd turned her head away, and D'Haven retracted his hand though he didn't want to.

"So, um… you have any plans now that you're a free man?" she asked.

Leaning against the island in the kitchen, D'Haven shrugged. "A few. First thing is finding a job." That made Astryd smile.

"I know a few places that are hiring if you're interested. I mean, I know it's not something you're used to, but it's a start."

"That's a'ight. This is a brand-new start for me. A clean slate Pebbles," he said casually making Astryd blush so hard.

"Oh, my goodness," she giggled. "I know you don't remember that silly nickname."

D'Haven grinned and licked his lips. "Of course, I do. I gave it to you. And, by the looks of it, it's still fitting."

A flush of heat covered Astryd's body as his eyes fell on what she knew were her hardened nipples.

That nickname was very fitting, and his intense stare was making her lady parts thump uncontrollably.

"Stop," she let out almost breathlessly.

"Stop what?"

"Staring at me like you're going to eat me alive."

"I could if you want me to," he said easily. "I wouldn't mind at all, and you know that. But I don't think your man would approve."

Astryd didn't like the way he made that last remark. Though Alonzo wasn't shit, she would never let someone else bad mouth him. Though that was far from what D'Haven was doing, the barrier she had temporarily let down in his presence was back up.

"Actually, he wouldn't. Not that my man is any of your business," she sassed.

"He's not, and clearly you're not his. What man lets his woman come to another man's welcome home party, knowing she was once in love with him?"

Astryd's eyes stretched widely. "That was years ago."

"Time has no limit on what the heart feels. Trust me, I know."

Stepping close in her space, Astryd held her

breath as his face lowered to her cheek. His closeness was about to make her lose her mind and the flood that had gathered between her legs leak. When he spoke in her ear with his minty fresh breath, she could have floated to the pearly gates.

"You look good as fuck by the way. Thank you for blessing me with your presence and welcoming me home."

With his words sealed by a kiss to her cheek, D'Haven pulled back and headed for the door he entered through. Breathless, Astryd stood in place rapidly blinking her eyes. *What in the world was that?* She had to ask herself the question. After years of Alonzo being the only man whose lips touched any part of her body, they felt nothing like D'Haven's. The simple kiss set off fireworks in her core that expanded through her chest.

Grabbing ahold of it, Astryd couldn't believe how fast her heart was beating. The pace it was pumping couldn't be safe. Picking up her wine, she chugged it down in a few gulps, exhaled, and chuckled.

"I have to stay away from him."

The words sounded good coming from her lips, but D'Haven wasn't going to let her. Their brief encounter had him wanting to be in her presence more than she knew. Was it the best decision to be knowing she had a man? Absolutely not. Did he care about her relationship? To an extent, yes, but he cared about Astryd more, and the energy she gave off wasn't sitting right with him. Until he figured out why, D'Haven was going to make it his duty to be wherever she was. Little did he know, Astryd didn't go anywhere but to work and home. Keeping up with her would be a task; one he'd gladly take on.

Later that evening, his mind was still on her as he stroked the insides of Baylei's walls. She wasn't as tight as he would have preferred, but she was wet as hell, so she'd have to do. The way she sucked his dick had D'Haven wishing he hadn't even slid a rubber on and entered her; the head could have been enough.

"Aaah, yes. Right there," Baylei moaned loudly.

Squeezing his eyes shut, D'Haven forced himself to drown out her moans, and imagine Astryd's. The girl was driving him crazy already, and he hadn't been home twenty-four hours yet.

He imagined the curve of her hips, lips, and ass from early that day. She was fully clothed and still looked better than all the scantily-clad women in attendance. The way her cheekbones lifted when she giggled invaded his mind and then it drifted to her nipples. Her pebbles that he had once wrapped his thick lips around and had the pleasure of tasting.

Though it had been years, the image of her young body back then had gotten him through more than a few lonely nights in jail. The smell of her hair, the soft moans she released in his ear, the way she clawed at his back plagued his memory and before he knew it, D'Haven was releasing his seeds into the condom with Astryd on his mental.

Groaning, he nutted for so long, he thought he'd never stop. Breathing hard, he pulled out of Baylei with ease and sat back on the bed. Swiping her hair from her face, Baylei grinned up at his rock-hard abs and flaccid covered dick. It was bigger than she remembered, but she wasn't complaining at all.

"Damn, that was good," she let out.

Climbing out the bed, D'Haven didn't give her a response. It was good, but he was ready to head home. It'd been a long day and would be an even longer one tomorrow. After flushing the condom and washing his hands, he walked back into the room. Slipping his jeans and tee on, Baylei stared at him with a bewildered expression masking her pretty face.

"It's three in the morning, D'Haven. I know you're not leaving."

"I'm getting dressed for a reason, B," was all he offered.

She sat completely up in the bed. "Why? You can stay the night. I can get up and cook breakfast for you like old times."

"That's the thing... this ain't old times. I don't want you thinking because I'm a free man now and tossed you some dick that this is more than what it was. You and I both know we could never go back to that."

Baylei's eyes watered. That was not what she was trying to hear. "I know I wasn't there for you, and I'm sorry. Why can't we just start over? You don't have to leave."

"And you should never beg a nigga to stay. Starting over would be pointless and will never happen with us."

D'Haven wasn't about to explain to her how her hoeish ways were one of the reasons they could never be again. It was her disloyalty as his woman back then that really had him not wanting to deal with her. Sliding between her legs shouldn't have caused any confusion, but he should've known better. Instead of Baylei taking the dick as a way of him releasing years of built up sexual frustration, she took it as them getting back together. That was never happening.

"Is this because I fucked Tech? I'm a big girl, you can tell me."

D'Haven chuckled. "Nah. If you thought giving him the pussy was a good move, that's on you. It's just pussy, B. He gone always be my nigga. I'm leaving because I have business to handle in the morning and it doesn't involve being laid up over here. Come lock up," he said smoothly, snatching his keys from her dresser.

D'Haven had never talked to Baylei so disrespectfully, and her heart broke the second those cold words left his mouth. "How could you say that to me? L-Like I don't mean shit to you!" she yelled at his back.

"You don't."

His answer was so dry, Baylei gasped. Picking up the closest object to her, the remote, she launched it at his head, but it hit his back instead. "Fuck you!"

D'Haven turned and faced her with the coldest look in his eyes. He didn't play that hitting shit. "Don't ever in your life throw something at me. If I knock your ass upside your fucking head, you'd be ready to call the cops. Let me get the fuck up outta here 'fore I be back in jail," he grumbled making his way out of her bedroom and the front door.

He didn't care if she locked it or not anymore. Hopping in his ride, D'Haven ran his hands down his head. Thinking with the wrong head this time around had him irritated. She knew better than to ever think they'd be in a relationship again. The notion was absurd, honestly. D'Haven would much rather settle down once he got his shit together. The person he'd settle down with would be a good wholesome woman. One who had her head on straight and could encourage him on the days he didn't feel encouraged at all.

Thinking back to Astryd offering to give him a few jobs that were hiring, D'Haven smiled. She was eager to help him get back on his feet, and he loved that. Grabbing his phone out the cup holder, he didn't care about it being three in the morning as he scrolled to his cousin's name in his new phone. There weren't many contacts, so Honey's name was quick to get to. The text he sent was simple yet had him feeling nervous as hell. Asking for Astryd's number was risky knowing Honey would probably never give it up, but it was worth a shot. A shot he was willing to take and miss if he had to.

Chapter Four

"I hope he likes it!" Ashlee squealed, as she decorated the cake in front of her.

Today was Alonzo's birthday, and instead of the family going out to eat to celebrate, Astryd opted on having dinner at home. It was prepared with love from the girls and her assistance. He had been in a good mood all week which was a surprise to her, and she wanted to keep it that way.

"He will baby. Put a little more on this side, and we're done," Astryd pointed out as Ashlynn waddled around the kitchen. She still hadn't grown out of her chunky legs, and it was the cutest thing seeing her bowlegged walk.

The girls had prepared Alonzo's favorite meal; fried chicken, greens, cornbread, macaroni and cheese, and a chocolate cake. Astryd had texted him an hour ago asking when he'd be home and instead of his usual rude reply, he gave her a time. Looking at the time on the stove, they had about ten minutes until he arrived.

"Daddy will be here in a minute. Let's get cleaned up so we can grab his gifts," she said, helping Ashlee down from the chair she was standing in at the counter.

Once they were cleaned up and sitting at the table with candles lit, they waited anxiously for their daddy to walk in the door. Despite the abuse he handed out to their mother like a free hug, his daughters loved him immensely. Ashlee was smitten with everything he did, and it broke Astryd's heart to see the sad look on her face when an hour passed by and Alonzo hadn't shown up yet.

"He isn't coming?" she asked softly with a hopeful look in her eyes.

Astryd swallowed down the ache in her throat. "He's just running late. You ready to eat?"

"Yes!" Ashlynn said clapping her little palms together.

Ashlee's head dropped, and Astryd hurriedly stood from the table so her daughter wouldn't see the tear she shed. It was one thing to hurt her, but to stand her babies up when they had been anticipating surprising him on his funky ass day was another thing. As she fixed their plates, Astryd called Alonzo's phone only for it to go straight to voicemail. That let her know that he had turned his phone off, but for what?

When the girls were done eating, Astryd not touching a single serving of food, she gave them a bath and tucked them in bed. Softly, she sang them the song her mother would sing her, and Ashlynn was out like a light. Ashlee yawned as her eyes fluttered.

"Mommy," she called out.

"Yes, Pumpkin?"

"Can you wake me up when Daddy gets here? I want to give him my gift."

Astryd wanted to break down, but she kept her cool. "You can give it to him in the morning okay?"

Sleepily, she nodded her head. Leaning her way, Astryd placed a single kiss to her forehead and squeezed her eyes together. Her babies were innocent and didn't deserve the hurt Alonzo was inflicting upon them at a young age. Ashlynn was only two, but Ashlee was old enough to convey her feelings, and tonight baby girls were crushed.

Cracking the door to their bedroom, Astryd

made her way downstairs and took a seat at the table. It was now nine-thirty-one. Two hours and thirty-one minutes past the time Alonzo said he'd be home. Anger consumed Astryd at his blatant disrespect, then sadness consumed her body as if it was all it knew. Stumped at the realization of him standing his family up on what was supposed to be a good day, Astryd placed her elbows on the table and her head in her palms.

Once the first tear broke free, the rest followed in an unbroken stream. Softly, she whimpered at the unspeakable pain Alonzo was causing her. Her mental was ruined, and he had done it with ease. He had broken her spirit and sheltered it, so no one would be able to heal her in any way. She was his. His to hurt, to diminish, to patronize, to bruise and his to love the only way he wanted her to be loved; conditionally.

After another hour of waiting, silently crying and halfway sleep, Astryd heard the front door open, and her head popped up. Quickly, she wiped the tears from her face, swallowed down any ill feelings, and ran her hands through her hair. Standing up, she adjusted the tight-fitting dress she slipped on just for him and cleared her throat as he rounded the corner.

"Yeah, I'm here. Nah, not tonight. I'ma fuck with you later," Alonzo said as he walked into the kitchen. Seeing Astryd in her small dress, makeup on, and looking like every bit of his birthday gift, she expected him to at least give her a grin, but he didn't.

Her heart dropped to the soles of her feet as he bypassed her and went straight to the stove to pick up a piece of chicken. Dumbfounded, Astryd licked her lips and turned his way as he continued his phone conversation.

"I said I'ma fuck with you tomorrow, damn. Bye."

Sliding his phone into his pocket, he turned around while smacking loudly. His eyes were red, and his outfit was different from the one he had left out in. Sliding his arm around her waist, Alonzo pulled her to him and gripped her ass.

"You got all dressed up for me?"

She nodded. "I did. The girls and I made you dinner, and you bailed on us, Zo. I told you to be here at 7."

"You told me or asked me to be here?"

"I asked you to. We wanted to spend your day with you, and you pop up three hours later. That's not fair."

Taking a bit of his chicken, he chewed and pecked her lips. "I'm sorry, ma. Some shit came up."

When she inhaled, the scent of a sweet perfume invaded her nose. Something had come up alright, and it wasn't an emergency. Refusing to break down in front of him, Astryd sighed and tucked her feelings away like she had been doing to save face or a beat down.

"It's fine. Do you want me to fix you a plate?"

His hand dropped from her waist. "Nah. I'm good. I already ate. You can cut me a piece of that cake though and bring it to me."

Once his demand was made, Alonzo strolled out of the kitchen to their room. Disappointment filled Astryd at lightning speed. She thought about spitting on his damn cake and tossing it in the trash. But, that wouldn't fix anything. It'd surely make things worse. After cutting him a piece, Astryd climbed the steps and walked into their bedroom. Alonzo was sitting up in the bed on his phone but looked up when she was in front of him. Grinning, he grabbed the plate.

"Thanks, baby."

"You're welcome," she said, before turning and walking away.

"Dang. That's it?" He called it out like she forgot something, and she had. Turning slowly on the balls of her feet, she faced him.

"Happy Birthday," she said dryly.

"It'll be an even better one once you bring your ass to bed. Clean that shit up downstairs and hurry back to your man."

Astryd rolled her eyes so hard once she was down the hallway, they could have gotten stuck. Had they, she'd be glad to not have to see his face anymore. As she packed away the food and wiped the counters down, her phone vibrated against the granite. Brows pinched, Astryd stared at the unknown numbers text message that popped up. She had it set to where her phone didn't show the message, so she had to open it to see what it said. When she did, a hand quickly covered her mouth.

+1 (816) 555-0127: `Pebbles, I know it's late, but I just wanted to invite you out for my birthday. You do remember when that is right? Have a good night beautiful.`

OF COURSE, she remembered when it was. It was a day after Alonzo's. The reason she was doing everything in her power to give him a memorable birthday, so her mind wouldn't be on what D'Haven was doing to celebrate his first birthday out of jail. Her fingers stammered over the keyboard, anticipating sending him a reply.

She wanted to so badly but knew she couldn't. Not right now at least. Them reconnecting wouldn't end well. Nothing in her life seemed to end well, and before she played a dangerous game of back and forth with D'Haven, she'd block his number. And, that's exactly what she did.

"How did he get my number anyway?" she said softly and shook her head.

Deleting the message altogether, she locked her phone and continued cleaning up the kitchen but quickly remembered she was supposed to give D'Haven a package from Winston. Sucking her teeth, she promptly sent Honey a text and asked if they could meet up tomorrow, so she could send it through her instead. Astryd wanted to keep her distance from D'Haven for as long as possible. It was safe. Safer than the danger she'd put herself in had she given into her urges to see him.

SITTING at the foot of the bed with a scowl on his face, Alonzo's eyes roamed Astryd's body in the tight, cream-colored dress adorning her frame. Thoughts of bending her over before she left out with her girls invaded his mind, but just as quickly as those thoughts came, they left.

"You need to change," he said sternly.

Whipping her head around to face him, Astryd's perfect brows indented her forehead. "What?"

"You heard what the fuck I said."

Swallowing the lump in her throat, Astryd said, "What's wrong with my dress?"

"It's too fucking short... and why am I explaining myself to you?" He hissed. "Change out that shit before you be staying here. Yo' ass been going out too much any fucking way. Let me find out you messing around on me."

The growl in his voice caused a chill to cover Astryd's frame. As she walked into their closet, a frown was on her face. She didn't want to change. Getting dolled up made her feel beautiful though on the inside she felt everything but. The little number she was rocking showcased her long legs and made her breasts sit up lovely. Her hair cascaded down her back in its natural curly state. The light makeup she applied gave her skin a shimmery glow she used to naturally have.

Pouting, she snatched a pair of black jeans down. Tugging the dress over her head, careful not to mess up her face, she tossed it to the ground and slid the jeans on. Huffing, she swiped through her expensive threads that didn't mean a thing to her. They never did. Stumbling across a sleeveless white sheer top that crisscrossed in the front. Astryd removed her tan bra for a black one. Her mother made it very clear the appropriate color undergarments to wear with what type of clothing. She absolutely hated when women wore colored bras with white shirts or colored underwear with white pants. Stepping out of the closet, she ran smack dab into Alonzo who was leaning against the sink.

Licking his lips, he eyed her lustfully. "You getting thick."

Self-consciously, Astryd tugged on the front of her shirt. She didn't even have a reply to that. Alonzo didn't say it as a compliment, though his eyes said otherwise. Astryd knew he was saying it to be condescending.

"This better?" She asked instead.

"Yeah. Where you say y'all was going again?"

She shrugged. "I'm not sure. Honey said it was a surprise. Something about celebrating me getting a slight raise at my job."

Alonzo nodded. "Yeah… aight. You need to text me and let me know where y'all going, who all there and be home by midnight."

"Alonzo," Astryd sighed.

"Alonzo what? You ain't about to stay out all night while I'm in the house. Fuck you think this is?"

"You can go out, it's not like I'm keeping you on a timer the way you—"

SLAP!

The smack to her face came so quickly, Astryd honestly didn't know what hit her. Hastily, Alonzo pushed himself up from the counter and gripped her face in his hands so hard, Astryd whimpered.

"You better watch your mothafuckin' mouth. You my bitch. Not the other way around. Now, what time you gon' have yo' ass back in this house?" he spat.

"Midnight," Astryd mumbled.

Mushing her hard into the wall, Alonzo glared down at her. "That's what I thought I said."

When he walked out of the bathroom, Astryd blinked back tears and placed a hand against her chest. The fear of him doing much more almost crippled her. A smack to the face was nothing compared to the incident that happened a few weeks ago. The thought of puking on her own now was traumatic. Inhaling, she released a hard breath and stepped up to the counter. Thankfully, the makeup she had on caused for his handprint to not bruise her skin this time around. Grabbing a towel, Astryd dabbed underneath her eyes and applied her nude lip gloss.

Regardless of the bullshit she was going through at home, she wasn't about to pass up the opportunity to celebrate life. A life she cherished but gambled with every day. Back in the bedroom, she slid on her leather, dark orange ankle booties. They matched perfectly with her orange snakeskin clutch. Looking at her phone, a text popped up from Honey letting her know she was a few minutes away.

"See you later," she mumbled to Alonzo.

"Come give me a kiss."

Obediently, though she didn't want to, Astryd marched over to his side of the bed. Pecking his lips, he smacked her ass and smirked.

"I'm sorry for putting my hands on you, a'ight."

Are you? Is what she wanted to say, but instead Astryd just nodded her head.

"Don't have too much fun and remember what the fuck I said."

Astryd gave him a forced smile. "I won't."

Before leaving out, Astryd peeked in on her girls. They were both knocked out early for a Friday night. After placing a kiss on each of their foreheads, she made her way outside. The sounds of Trina blasted in Honey's car and put a smile on Astryd's face when she opened the door and climbed inside.

"Oh. It's one of those nights?" She laughed.

"Yes! You see this outfit bitch? I'm killing you hoes," Honey rapped, putting her car in reverse. "You look fiiine, friend!"

"Thank you, girl. I had on a dress but decided to change at the last minute."

She'd never tell her Alonzo made her change. Astryd and Honey had been best friends for years, but still, she was fearful of letting her in on that part of her life. It wasn't an attribute she was proud of at all.

"That's fine. You'll get in with jeans on," Honey replied.

"Where are we going anyway? You swear it's top secret."

Chuckling, Honey shot her friend a sly grin. "It was because I knew you would probably decline. D'Haven is having a party at the club for his birthday."

Astryd's entire body heated. "W-What. I thought we were celebrating my raise?"

"We are. We're just gonna celebrate with him, too. That's cool, right? We can go somewhere else. I just figured going out to eat would be kind of boring."

Looking out the window, Astryd thought about the text D'Haven had sent her earlier in the week. He had invited her out for his birthday, but she thought he meant that day. But, of course, he was doing it big. It was his first birthday not behind bars in five years; he wasn't just celebrating for one day.

"No, no. That's cool. It's been a while since I've been to the club," she replied.

"Good! I'm ready to get drunk," Honey giggled. "Everyone is going to be there, too."

Astryd's stomach flip-flopped. She was beyond nervous to see D'Haven again, but a part of her was excited as well. She didn't plan to get drunk like Honey planned to do, but she knew she'd definitely need a few drinks to make it through the night. And, that's exactly what she did once they made it to the club.

Club Monarch was packed. From the parking lot to the inside, it was full of people who had either been invited to celebrate with D'Haven or were just there trying to enjoy the night. Either way, the vibe was off the chain.

"Can we go to the bar?"

"We don't need to stand at the bar. D'Haven has bottles in his section," Honey said in her ear.

"Oh, okay. I didn't know."

"Yeah, girl. He wants all his people to just enjoy themselves. No spending money which I'm not complaining about one bit," she laughed.

Making their way to his section, Astryd was approached three times before she could even make it up the steps to their people. That thickness Alonzo didn't appreciate was highly appreciated by the men in the club. And when they finally made it to D'Haven's section, it seemed as if all eyes were on her as well.

"Aye. That's Astryd?" Tech asked, tapping D'Haven twice with the back of his hand.

Lifting up from pouring himself a drink, D'Haven let his eyes scan the area until they landed on her.

Astryd was hugging Greigh, and then Lee before embracing their men. Seeing her smile made him grin. When his eyes trailed her frame, he shook his head.

"Damn," he hissed lowly… appreciatively.

With the number of half-dressed ass women who had approached him since he arrived, it was nice to see her fully clothed and still killing most of the women inside.

"Yeah, that's her. Surprised she came out," he said more to himself.

"You know you bringing the people out," Tech said, drinking from his cup.

They had been on brown all night, and it was still early. Blunts were being passed around D'Haven's homeboys while the ladies sipped from flutes filled with liquor. He wanted to celebrate his freedom and chill in the house, which he did on the day of his birthday, but Tech made him step out tonight. It was the last year of his twenties, and his boy was going to make sure he lived that shit up.

"Cousin," Honey grinned walking over to him. "Happy Birthday!"

Hugging her, D'Haven chuckled. "Thanks, cuz. You know my shit was on Monday, right?"

"And? You get to celebrate all month, hell.

Don't start. Look who I brought," she said before leaning closer. "Guess me giving you her number didn't work out so well, huh?"

"Man, watch out," he chuckled. "What's up Pebbles."

Astryd smiled softly though she wanted to grin wide at the pet name. "Hey. Happy birthday.," she said stepping closer to him.

D'Haven hugged her tightly and whispered in her ear, "You get my text?"

"Um, yeah. I forgot to reply."

That was a smooth lie. She wanted to reply but didn't have the courage to do so. D'Haven knew it too. Her poker face wasn't shit.

"It's all good. Glad you could come show love. You look good," he complimented, letting his eyes roam her frame.

"Thank you. How old are you now old man?" she laughed comfortably.

Laughing, smiling and being herself around D'Haven came naturally. Tugging at the hair on his chin, D'Haven chuckled.

"Old man? Damn like that?"

His handsome smirk made all the jitters in Astryd's body reappear.

"I'm twenty-nine. That'd make you what now... twenty-six?"

Astryd nodded. "Yep. Still a baby."

"Nah," he countered. "You're far from a baby."

Astryd quivered. His intense, dreamy stare had her freaking out.

"Still got a cute baby face though."

She swatted his arm, hitting nothing but firm muscle. "Oh, whatever. You mind if I get a drink?"

You mind if I get a drink of you? Is what D'Haven wanted to ask her. He was damn near parched from having this conversation with Astryd and needed her to quench his thirst. She asked so politely, it made his dick hard. She was a good girl, still. He could tell, but something in her eyes was troubling her spirit. Even in his almost drunken state, D'Haven could peep the facade she had up.

"Go ahead. Drink whatever."

Hearing those words, Astryd eagerly grabbed a flute and filled it with Patron, before adding some orange juice to it. D'Haven had his eyes trained on her as she took the first sip. When she exhaled the breath she seemed to be holding in, he grinned at the pleasant smirk on her face.

"What?" she questioned.

"Just admiring your beauty is all. Can I do that?"

Bashfully, Astryd ran a hand through her curls. D'Haven didn't have to ask, but she was glad he had. He was making her nervous again but in a good way. Taking a huge gulp of her drink, she nodded her head.

"Yeah, sure," she replied just as Baylei and Demi walked up.

Purposely, Baylei bumped Astryd causing her to swivel in her direction.

"My fault girl. I had too much to drink," Baylei offered up.

Though she and Demi had indulged in one too many shots before they headed to the club, that wasn't the reason she bumped into her. Seeing Astryd all in her ex's face had her hot. The way D'Haven was looking in his crisp white button down with the top two unbuttoned, thin gold chain around his neck, tattooed arms on display and fresh line, Baylei wasn't going for any female besides her being in his face. She didn't give a damn if it was his party or not.

Astryd gave her a simple once over and focused her attention back on D'Haven. "I'll come say bye before I leave."

"Aight. Don't make me have to look for you, woman," he replied making her blush.

"I won't."

"Hey, girl. Your man let you out the house tonight?" Demi said playfully, but in reality, it was the truth.

Alonzo had let her out, and if he knew where she was at, all hell would break loose. Giving her a shrug Astryd said, "Yeah, sure."

The mention of Alonzo had Astryd gulping down her drink as she walked away. She didn't want to have him on her mind, especially when she knew she had lied to him about her whereabouts. D'Haven peeped the flustered look on her face and frowned, and his frown only deepened when Baylei openly rubbed her hand against his crotch. D'Haven smacked her hand away.

"Aye, watch out. I ain't fucking with you like that," he told her.

"Why? Because of her?"

"Nah, because of you. I don't have to explain myself to you Baylei," he chuckled, picking is cup up from the table.

"Whatever. You lucky I don't show out up here."

"Go ahead. You gon' be getting put right the

fuck out. Matter fact, you can leave for real. I ain't really feeling your presence right now."

Baylei's jaw dropped. "What? What the fuck is that supposed to mean? I was invited!"

"By my sister. Before you start trying to make a scene, just leave man. I ain't in the mood for your ass."

With that, D'Haven walked away to mingle with his folks. Baylei was trying her best to get back in his good graces, but her attempts were falling short. With an attitude written all over her face, Baylei roughly made her a drink and quickly tossed it back. She couldn't believe the way D'Haven was handling her. Yes, she had fucked his niggas, but she thought they'd at least still be friends. He didn't even want to be that, honestly. Feeling herself tear up, Baylei shook her head and faced Demi.

"You ready to go?"

Demi frowned. "We just got here ten minutes ago. You can leave, but I'm not ready yet."

"Fine, but I'm going downstairs to find me a new nigga. Your brother acting all stuck up and shit," she fussed.

Demi waved her off. "Okay, girl. If that's what you think. I'll text you when I'm ready to go."

Baylci rolled her eyes and walked off. Sometimes, she asked herself why she was even friends with Demi's ass, then she remembered she had gotten close to her just so she could fuck D'Haven and make herself his girl. Her plan went through, but it was over now. D'Haven wasn't checking for her ass anymore.

Across the section, Astryd was tossing back a strong shot of something Honey wouldn't reveal. It went down smooth as hell, but that wasn't the point. Sticking her tongue out, her body shivered once the drink was in her system.

"Okay, no more shots for me," she announced.

"You have to take one more. That was for your raise, the next one is for D'Haven's birthday," Honey said as her man, Jamir, handed her a shot of something clear.

"I ain't drinking no clear shit," Esmin griped. "Where the Remy at?"

"Oh no. You gon' drink this Patron tonight," Greigh said making her girls chuckle. Leaning over she whispered in her man's ear. "You a beast off that Tequila, Daddy."

Esmin smacked her ample ass. "I'ma beast period. You just better be ready to toot that ass up on this dick and give me another baby."

"Gladly," Greigh grinned, smooching his lips.

"Y'all are so cute," Lee smiled. "Aren't they bae?"

"Nah. You the only cute thing I see for real," Demir replied draping his arm over her shoulder and pulling her into his side.

"Oh my gosh," Honey squealed. "Y'all are so mushy. I know y'all drunk."

"Nope. This is how we always are," Lee answered for her and Greigh. Her friend had her tongue down Esmin's throat, and she was sure she'd be carrying baby number two real soon.

Once Honey had everyone's attention, she gave a special birthday shout-out to her cousin, welcomed him home again, and everyone tossed their shot back. A few people were drinking straight from the bottle, and D'Haven was one of them. The Hennessy had him feeling lovely. He didn't even have the urge to smoke anymore, which in his case, was a good thing. His PO was an asshole and told him straight up that he'd be making him drop come Monday morning.

While everyone grooved to the music and caught up, Astryd stepped over to the railing and looked out at the sea of dancing bodies. She had reached her limit and couldn't stop twirling her hips. She felt free. A feeling she hadn't felt in so long, she didn't know what to do. The DJ set the mood just right as Astryd swayed to the smooth sound of Caramel by Lloyd. When she felt a strong pair of hands wrap around her waist, she froze up.

"No need to stop now," D'Haven whispered in her ear. "Gon' dance for me with your sexy ass."

Astryd's knees buckled, but his hold on her kept her from collapsing. The liquid courage crept up on Astryd in a rush. The feel of him enclosed around her frame, warm breath against her neck, and bulge in his pants against her ass, had her feeling bold. With confidence, she began to move her body like an exotic dancer to the beat. With each dip of her back and twirl of her hips, D'Haven was right there with her catching every move she made. Moving her hair from her neck, he placed a soft kiss against it, and the seat of Astryd's thong flooded.

"D-D'Haven," she whispered out in a tremble.

"Yeah Pebbles?"

"You can't kiss on me like that," she breathed out.

Ignoring her, D'Haven licked her neck and pulled her closer to his body. His hand caressed her belly as she stopped moving. Hell, she was hardly breathing as well. When his hand slid up her shirt, somehow, his warmth caused her to shiver. Chills covered her exposed arms as he did whatever it was he was doing to her body. He was making it his own without properly asking permission, but Astryd didn't give a damn.

"I wanna eat your pussy so bad," he admitted in a gentle, sonorous tone. He said it as if it were an everyday task like brushing his teeth. D'Haven wanted to make it a daily task on his to-do list and place a check by it when complete. He made a promise to do it well too, if she'd let him.

Astryd couldn't find her voice. He snatched it away the moment he placed those soft, juicy lips against her neck. Though vulgar as hell, his admission of wanting to taste her were the most endearing words ever. She was so turned on if D'Haven whispered another word in her ear, she was liable to orgasm on the spot.

"I hope I'm not interrupting anything," someone called out from behind them.

Astryd didn't realize her eyes were closed until they popped open at the sound of that voice. Maneuvering from D'Haven's grasp, she squealed and jumped into her big brother's open arms.

"Winston! Oh my gosh! I didn't know you were coming home," she said feeling slighted.

"That's the point of surprises, baby girl. Happy to see me?"

Drunkenly, Astryd pinched his cheek. "Of course, I am. I swear you look like your daddy the older you get."

The siblings had the same mother, but different dads. While Winston didn't possess Astryd's foreign looks, he was still as handsome as ever. Smooth skin the color of cognac, a clean low-cut fade, and a ripped body like the football coach he was, Winston didn't lack in looks at all. Astryd was surprised he hadn't brought any kids home yet. His answer was always, I'm focused on me right now, kids can wait. And, they could until he was ready to settle down. Until then, he was going to continue to spoil his nieces as if they were his own.

"That dude looks like me," he chuckled before he and D'Haven slapped hands. "My guy. Welcome home, baby."

Embracing one another, their manly greeting that lasted longer than a usual hug made tears come to Astryd's eyes. The sacrifices made on D'Haven's behalf to keep her brother out of jail were the reason for the heartfelt greeting. In his last year of undergrad, and a scholarship underway with plans to attend graduate school, Winston got caught slipping, and Astryd felt like it was all her fault.

Three months into her relationship with Alonzo back in 2013, he flipped out and punched Astryd for asking a simple question. She had caught wind of him fucking around with a girl from their city, but instead of assuming, she brought it to him. When she didn't get the answer she liked and said something slick out of her mouth, a swift punch was delivered right after. Stunned by his actions, the first thing Astryd did was call her brother.

Hearing his sister sobbing into the phone had Winston ready to kill Alonzo on sight. At the time, he was home from school and kicking it with D'Haven. When Winston let him know what was going on, they dropped what they had planned and headed to Alonzo's crib, but got pulled over on the way there. Winston had a gun in the console and quickly panicked not knowing what to do. When the cops instructed them to get out and came back with the gun and some drugs questioning them, D'Haven spoke up and claimed the weapon as his.

Not wanting to see Winston throw his life away for a petty gun charge, D'Haven took the charge for him. Instead of the few years he thought he was going to sit down, the judge gave him the max because he already had a previous misdemeanor on his record. D'Haven felt it was the right thing to do and didn't regret it. The only person who felt remorseful was Astryd. In her mind, had she not called him to come get her, he and D'Haven wouldn't have gotten pulled over.

It was the past now though, and D'Haven was home. He wasn't into dwelling on his past transgressions in life. Those years behind bars taught him to appreciate everything positive when there was so much negativity in the world. Had he not wanted to claim the gun as his, he wouldn't have. He was a man about his and seeing the man Winston had become over the years was worth it. He held his boy down the entire time and blessed his pockets with the gift Astryd sent through Honey.

"'Preciate you. You buff as hell ain't you?" D'Haven jested.

"Them weights dawg. You about to bust out yo damn shirt. Got my sis over here with stars in her eyes," Winston laughed, pulling Astryd into his side and kissing her forehead. "You drunk?"

She nodded softly with a smile. "Mhm."

"You drove?"

Winston was playing the big brother role like only he could. With him being away most of the time, he cherished the moments he did share with Astryd.

"No, I rode with Honey. I have to be home at midnight though," she said before her eyes popped open and realization hit her.

Scrambling through her clutch for her phone, Astryd felt every drop of liquor she drank ready to spew from her lips. The time on her cell phone staring back at her read 11:49. She was having such a good time; the time had slipped away from her. She knew there was no way she was going to make it home in eleven minutes.

"Why midnight?" Winston asked.

"Ashlee has a dance recital in the morning. I gave myself a curfew," she giggled nervously. She was so swift with her lies, Winston didn't even peep the tremor in her voice.

"You'll be good to wake up. Just drink some water and take a BC powder before you go to sleep," Winston told her.

Astryd swallowed the ache in her throat, and her pride slid right down with it. She wanted to tell her brother, or someone, so badly about her abusive home life but couldn't. After the incident with Alonzo hitting her the first time, Astryd was going to leave him for good but found out she was pregnant. She couldn't believe how her life had turned out back then, and to this day, she was still in disbelief. But, her circumstances were only going to change if she wanted them to. No one else could make that decision for her and though it was scary, sometimes facing your fears is the only option when trying to survive. She was either going to sink or swim and right now she was on the verge of drowning but her two floaties, Ashlee and Ashlynn, were holding her afloat.

As the time ticked by, the more petrified Astryd became. She thought of slipping away and calling a Lyft, but her friends nor D'Haven were letting her out of their sight. She really got out of the house, and they were taking full advantage of it. When it hit a little after one, she yawned, and Winston came over to where she was sitting.

"Sis, I'm headed out. I got a meeting in the morning. You need a ride home?"

Astryd jumped to her feet so quickly, she stumbled in the heels she was rocking. Catching her wobbly frame from behind, D'Haven chuckled.

"Slow down, Pebbles. He ain't gon' leave you."

"He better not. You sure it's not out the way?" she asked, and Winston shook his head no.

"Nah. Even if it was, I was still going to drop you off. D, you good?"

The men slapped hands. "Yeah. Shit, I'ma head out in a minute, too. Let everybody finish drinking then get some food or something."

"Aight. I'll hit yo line tomorrow so we can link up."

D'Haven agreed and lightly pulled Astryd back to him once she took one step in the direction of the stairs.

"Come here. I know you ain't leaving without telling me goodnight."

The way the words flowed from his lips to Astryd's ears made her stomach churn. There was a slight slur in them, but stern enough to let her know he didn't appreciate her trying to walk off. Though the sight of her walking away was a sight to see, he'd much rather get another view of her pretty face before he closed his eyes in a few hours.

Astryd locked eyes with him, and her heart fluttered. It was everything about the way D'Haven carried himself that had her considering staying by his side for the night. The rebellious spirit she once possessed was creeping up but didn't quite make it to the forefront of her mind.

"Goodnight, D'Haven," she said softly. Eyes fluttering from his intoxicating smell and aura. She felt high in his presence and not because of the weed smoke smothering their section.

Pulling her into his embrace, Astryd wrapped her arms around his neck as his hands slid down her back. He wanted to grip her ass in the palm of his hands and thought against it but did it anyway. Respectfully, but savagely as well, D'Haven caressed her ass and whispered in her ear so erotically, Astryd could have fainted.

"It was indeed a good night, Pebbles. Your presence was the best present of them all."

She chuckled at the line and removed herself from his embrace. D'Haven wanted to kiss her, but he had already done enough.

"Drive safely okay?"

"Tech driving, so I'm good. You stay looking out," he grinned.

"It's only right that I do," she said and gave him a soft smile before heading to tell her girls bye.

D'Haven's eyes were trained on her until he could no longer see the top of her curly head descending the steps. He had it bad, but so did she. Had he known the sacrifice she just made to stay longer in his presence, D'Haven would have driven her home himself. The entire ride to her crib,

Astryd looked at the time on the dashboard. What had her even more spooked was the fact that Alonzo hadn't called or texted her not once. That right there made her sick to her stomach.

"What time Ashlee dance recital start?" Winston asked as he pulled into the driveway.

"At 10:30. Want me to send you the information?"

Yeah. Text it to me. My meeting should be over around that time."

"Okay. Thank you for the lift home. I can't believe you snuck up on me," she grinned making him do the same.

"You know I gotta keep an eye on you."

"Mhm. I bet. I'll see you tomorrow."

He hit the locks. "Aight. Love you."

"Love you too. Drive safely, please."

"Always. I had one drink."

Satisfied with his answers, Astryd climbed out his car and moseyed to the front door. Winston didn't pull off until she was safely inside. With the kitchen light illuminating the hall, Astryd slipped her heels off and carried them in her hand up the steps. Her heart beat wildly in her chest the closer she got to their bedroom door. Palms sweating, she held on tightly to her heels and swallowed hard before walking inside. When she heard Alonzo's snores echoing lowly through the room, she released her breath and headed to the bathroom.

Afraid that the shower may wake him up, Astryd slipped out of her clothes, tossed on a big t-shirt, and climbed in the bed after relieving her bladder. Slowly, she scooted under the covers and laid her head down. After five minutes of laying there completely stiff, she closed her eyes. She was expecting the worst to happen from disobeying his orders, but tonight was her lucky night. With her only thoughts on D'Haven and the way she felt in his arms tonight, Astryd drifted off into a peaceful sleep.

The following morning, instead of Astryd's alarm waking her up like she planned for it too, Ashlee was her alarm clock. Stomping her little feet across the wood floor in her parents' room, Ashlee stood at the side of her mother's bed and gently shoved her shoulder.

"Mommy."

Astryd didn't budge. Shoving her harder this time, Astryd stirred from her inebriated sleep.

"Mommy wake up. We have to get ready for my recital."

Groaning, Astryd rolled over on her side and

peeled her heavy eyelids open. After a few blinks, she smiled softly at her baby girl.

"What time is it Pumpkin?" she questioned.

"Time to get up. It's my big day."

With glee, Ashlee did a few twirls and gave her mother a huge grin. Dancing had been her favorite pastime, and Astryd was more than willing to see to it that she stuck it out. It was hard on her at first being the youngest of the group, but her age didn't matter. Her instructors praised how she was more skilled than the older girls.

When Astryd lifted her body from the bed, confusion settled on her face. When Ashlee gave her the same expression, Astryd knew something was incredibly wrong.

"Whoa," Ashlee said in amazement. "You cut your hair, Mommy."

It wasn't a question but more of an observation. Astryd's lungs restricted, preventing her from speaking. Her tongue lied heavily in her mouth and hands violently shook as she brought one up to touch her now, bob length hair. Tears sprang to her eyes as she shot to her feet and ran to the bathroom. Inside, she gasped loudly and collapsed against the sink.

As her hands clenched the white porcelain, she

stared at her reflection in disbelief. Choppy, uneven layers of hair were what she had now. Gone was the luscious grade of hair she was so proud to call her own. It was a staple inherited from her mother. Her eyes blinked a few times before large tears dropped onto the sink.

"You don't like it?"

The sound of Alonzo's voice made her jump like always. Lackadaisically, he was leaned against the frame of the door with an evil smirk on his face.

"I think it's pretty!" Ashlee squealed, squeezing past him and standing next to Astryd at the sink.

Only because of her daughter, did Astryd not lash out at Alonzo. The smirk on his face was making her sick to her stomach. Her being hurt behind his repulsive action brought him joy. The tears staining her cheeks and gaze she held with him through the mirror made his dick hard. He got off on seeing her defeated. If she thought staying out all night had no repercussions, Alonzo quickly reminded her who the fuck was in charge.

"I don't," Astryd replied lowly.

Before she could take her next breath, Alonzo grabbed her by the back of her neck and squeezed so hard Astryd began to choke.

"Daddy!" Ashlee yelled, terrified.

Unmoved by her yelling, he squeezed down harder before shoving Astryd so hard, her body practically flew across the room. Not wanting Ashlee to see this type of behavior, Astryd quickly caught her balance and rushed to her. Through muffled words and an aching throat, she spoke slowly and carefully.

"G-Go to your room okay, baby?"

With fear and confusion in her big eyes, Ashlee blinked a few times. "You sure?"

Astryd nodded. It was the only thing she could do. If she tried speaking again, a cry would escape her lips instead of words. Guiding her to the door, Astryd tried to soothingly rub her back to calm her down, but it didn't work. Ashlee's heart was beating so fast, and she wanted to stay to protect her mother. When she looked toward Alonzo, he didn't even have the balls to face them. He was a coward for putting his hands on Astryd, to begin with, but to do it in front of their child was something Astryd wouldn't tolerate.

When Ashlee was out of their bedroom, and the door was locked, Astryd's body moved swiftly back into the bathroom.

"You walking in here like you about to do something," Alonzo chuckled. "Don't make me beat your ass."

"H-How could you do that? Why would you do that in front of her!" she hissed, as her words came out in a high-pitched tone.

"Why would you have another nigga all over you? Where the fuck did you go last night, and you better not lie."

"I told you where I went!" she screamed, unable to hold her anger in.

BAM!

The punch to her jaw caused Astryd's head to bang against the wall with force. Stars danced behind her eyelids as Alonzo's hand wrapped around her neck. Her feet dangled from the floor as he held her up against the wall.

"Bitch, who you think you talking to? Huh?" He spat, slamming her body into the towel bar. "You must want me to kill your hoe ass in here. Is that what you want?"

Without delay, Astryd shook her head from side to side.

"You been getting really bold lately. I don't know what nigga got you smelling yourself, but you better pipe the fuck down before your kids be raised by another woman and visiting your grave."

His threat was cold and stabbed Astryd right in the heart. Alonzo of all people knew how she felt regarding the subject of her mom and he used to it wound her. Tears rolled down her cheeks as he released her neck. Gasping, Astryd sucked in a deep breath. Air filled her aching lungs as Alonzo's words rang loudly in her ears. Her jaw was tender to touch, and the slight move from it was unbearable.

When Alonzo pulled her over to the sink, stood behind her, and tugged downward on her shorts, Astryd began to tell him not to even think about touching her, but she couldn't. Her beating would be much more brutal if she had.

"Now, I'ma ask you again. Where the fuck did you go last night?"

"Monarch," she said lowly, unable to raise her voice.

Alonzo nodded and forced her to bend over on the counter. "See, I already knew that, but you just had to lie huh? You had to come home with your fucking hair smelling like another niggas cologne and expect me to just let it fly?"

The tip of his dick against her flesh made Astryd cringe. She didn't want to answer him. No answer would be good enough. Roughly, he snatched her head back by her short, disheveled hair. Her roots were begging for him to loosen up some.

"Answer me!"

"No," she cried out. "Lonzo, please. Don't do this. I'm not even in the mood."

"You think I give a fuck about what mood you're in? When I want some pussy, my pussy, I'ma take it. Now arch your fucking back, and you better take all this dick."

Crying silently, Astryd bent over, and he roughly slammed into her unlubricated center. She was so turned off by him and everything he stood for, she didn't even care about letting him hear her cry. The harder he shoved into her, working up a sweat, the quicker his nut approached. Alonzo thought this was okay. He thought raping the mother of his kids and abusing her would make her love him. The days of loving him were long gone and had been for a while.

Feeling his nut creep up, Alonzo pulled out, yanked Astryd to her knees and ejaculated all in her hair. Going the extra mile, he rubbed the tip of his dick through her head and grinned.

"I bet you'll think twice before fucking around on me. Clean yourself up, and you better have my baby to her recital on time."

He didn't need to say or else, and she knew it. Had she gone against his orders this time around, Astryd was sure he'd go to extreme measures to degrade her even more. Pulling his shorts over his ass, Alonzo waltzed out of the bathroom and out their bedroom. Greeting him at the door was Ashlee. She had a hopeful look on her face as she stared up at him.

"Is Mommy okay?" she asked softly.

Alonzo gave her a smile and nodded. "Yes. She's in the shower."

"Why'd you push her?"

He wasn't expecting her to ask that question, but of course, he had an answer.

"I was mad, but I didn't mean to. It won't happen again, okay?"

She nodded. "Okay."

"You forgive me?"

She nodded again. "Yes. Can I still go to my recital?"

"Sure can. Go get dressed and be ready in twenty minutes."

"I'll be ready in ten!"

The excitement was back in her voice, and Alonzo was happy for that. He had blacked out for a second and held no regard for Ashlee seeing him in action. Him asking her for forgiveness and she willingly accepting it was the start of something disastrous.

In the shower, Astryd scrubbed her body before scratching her scalp so roughly, she was sure to have sores later. Every inch of her frame felt disgusting. His touch felt like a million tiny ants were crawling on her, burning her inside and out. Her thoughts ran rapid of his erratic, abusive behavior and how him hitting her started to happen more frequently. It was a behavior she didn't like at all. His statement on killing her and leaving her kids behind made a hyperventilating cry escape her lungs. Clinging onto the wall, Astryd cried from the depths of her soul. Though Alonzo claimed she was okay to Ashlee, she was everything but.

She was broken. Broken by a man who had provided her with a lifestyle and love so pure in the beginning, that when it started to turn sour, she just simply tolerated the acidic emotion. Astryd became immune to the hurt. There was no more begging him to love her right or asking him to respect not only her mind but her body as well. Stripping her of her confidence and pride, Alonzo had brought Astryd to her lowest. Remembering the look on her daughter's face is what made her rise from the low pit.

Lifting her head from the tile shower wall, Astryd peeled her eyes open and inhaled a deep breath. Today, she was going to make a change. The shift she had been waiting for was happening now, and she had no choice but to take advantage of it before it was too late. For her girls, she'd risk her life, but if she could keep it and them safe, she knew what she had to do.

Chapter Five

"Where are we?"

Ashlee's sleepy voice echoed through the entrance of the doorway they stood in. It had been three days since the incident in her bathroom, and far too many days since Alonzo first abused her. On a whim, no plan of action other than leaving her abusive relationship, Astryd picked her girls up from daycare before following the instructions given to her by an advocate.

Sunday morning, the day after Ashlee's recital, Astryd did a Google search on "Domestic Violence Shelters." To her surprise, many resources popped up. Even with Alonzo having been gone since Saturday morning after his assault, she still felt like he could see everything she was doing. Knowing it was her paranoia, Astryd wrote down a few of the numbers and called around to see what their programs were like.

Leaving Alonzo was the hard part. Finding a safe place to escape his wrath was even harder. He knew where everyone she was affiliated with stayed except for Greigh. She'd never place her friend's life in danger, nor her family, so she found the courage and reached out to shelters. When Monday rolled around, she had a list of three she was contemplating on calling again. On her lunch break today, Tuesday, she did just that. When she was accepted into one, Astryd left work early and sped to her home. Thankfully, there was no sign of Alonzo having set foot in the house since Saturday and Astryd thanked God for that.

Hastily, she packed she and her girls enough clothes without making it seem like she was gone. Though he'd see she was gone whenever he returned, she didn't want to make it too visible. After picking Ashlee up from daycare, she stopped by her Grammy's house to get Ashlynn.

Lola immediately noticed her uneasiness. She was surprised by her new cut on Saturday at the recital but was lost for words when her granddaughter revealed the truth about her and Alonzo's relationship. Like Astryd knew she would, Lola offered her to stay at her home, but she declined. Leaving was one thing, but her putting her Grammy in danger wasn't going to happen. Before she left to head to the shelter, Lola prayed with Astryd right there in the middle of her living room floor as her granddaughter cried hard.

After promising to call her once she was at her destination, one she couldn't reveal, Astryd and her girls headed to their new home. Now, here she was a ball of nerves with a hyper two-year-old ready to terrorize, and an inquisitive five-year-old by her side. It wasn't close to their bedtime at all, and with them being in a foreign place Astryd hoped they wouldn't be up half the night.

"Are you all hungry?" Lex, the advocate on duty, asked.

"No. We're fine."

"Okay. Well, let me show you around, and then we can start on your intake process before you get settled in. Is that okay?"

Astryd nodded as they walked through the hallway. "Yes."

Inside the office, Lex gave the girls coloring sheets and markers to keep busy while she and

Astryd went over the necessary paperwork. As she filled out her information, she blinked back tears as she answered some of the questions regarding Alonzo. Not because she felt sorry for him, but because she couldn't believe the shit he had really put her through. The questions were hard to answer, but she got through them. Her babies needed her to be strong right now and looking over at them as they colored and talked to each other, Astryd made a promise right then to them and herself. She wasn't going back no matter how hard things would get.

"Okay, I'm done," she sighed heavily.

"Great. Let me look through it, and then we'll head to your room."

After making sure all of the pages were filled out and answered, Lex showed Astryd and the girls to their room. She brought in three sets of towels, basic necessities, and blankets for them. It was a vast downsize from their rooms back home, but it was safe. That's all Astryd cared about.

"You need anything else before I head back to the office?" Lex asked.

"When can I meet with one of the case managers you mentioned?"

"More than likely tomorrow. They get in at

nine. You could meet after you take your girls to school."

Astryd scratched her head. "I'll more than likely keep them out for a few days. This is a big adjustment for us all, and I want to make sure they're comfortable."

"Of course. I understand completely. I'm here overnight if you need anything, even if you just want to talk, okay?"

Giving her a soft smile, something she hadn't done all week, Astryd nodded. "I will. Thank you so much for everything."

"You're more than welcome. Have a good night."

When the door closed, it seemed as if the walls of the room began to cave in. Sitting down on the bed, Astryd took in deep breaths to calm her nerves. She had left him. She didn't think this day would ever come, let alone happen. Their relationship taking a turn for the worst wasn't what Astryd had in mind when Alonzo first approached her. She saw them being together forever, at least in her mind and getting married. Living happily ever after like a fairy tale movie played in her mind back then as well, but their story didn't seem to be following the plot. Nothing about her life had been happy for a while now. The only thing that brought a smile to her face were her kids.

"Mommy?" Ashlee called out.

"Yes, baby?"

"Are you sad?"

Astryd choked back on a cry before placing Ashlee on her lap. "I was, but not anymore."

Ashlee gave her a big hug and kissed her cheek. "You don't have to be sad. It's okay. You have me and Ashlynn to cheer you up."

That brought a big smile to Astryd's face. "Of course, Pumpkin. You guys always cheer me up."

"Does Daddy cheer you up?"

He used to but not anymore, is what she wanted to say but opted not to. Regardless of the image he decided to show them, Astryd would never bad talk Alonzo to the girls. If they grew up despising him, it'd be from his own doing.

"Sometimes, yes," she replied as Ashlynn lifted her arms to be picked up.

"Okay."

Astryd's simple answer cured her curiosity for the moment, but she knew there'd be more questions where that one came from. The thing was, Astryd didn't know if she was ready to answer them. She could only hold herself accountable for her own actions. Her decision to flee her situation was the best one yet, too.

As Ashlynn nestled her face against her neck and yawned, Astryd rubbed her back and thanked God for granting her the strength to leave. Closing her eyes for a brief second, she thought what their days ahead would be like. She thought about her friends and how she'd finally explain to them the hell she had been living in for the last few years. It wasn't something she was proud about, but her escaping it reminded her of how brave she was. How strong she was to leave and how proud her mom would have been of her.

Astryd wanted everyone else to feel proud of her, but first, she had to be proud of herself. She needed to learn to love herself and remember the young woman she used to be before Alonzo selfishly tried to destruct her image. Learning to love herself more than anyone could was going to be the tough part, especially with the secrets she'd been harboring. In record speed, she had become an entirely different person and desperately wanted to get back to her old self. The process wasn't going to be easy, but she was going to trust it. That's all she could do.

STROLLING into work with her iced coffee in one hand, and phone in the other, Honey mentally prepared herself for the day. Walking into the main office, she greeted Lex with a smile.

"Good morning Sunshine," Lex greeted standing to her feet.

"Good morning. You look ready to go," Honey laughed.

She hadn't worked an overnight shift in so long, she was sure she'd be beyond tired once morning rolled around, too. Though she was a case manager, she covered the main hotline office for a few hours on Wednesday mornings, until the regular staff showed up at nine.

"I am. I'm hungry first of all," Lex chuckled.

"You should've texted me. I would've brought you some food."

"I'm heading straight home after this, so I'll grab something on the way. Let me give you an update so I can get out your way."

As Lex began giving her the shelter update starting with who was all in shelter, Honey grabbed the roster list. It was in chronological order beginning with the ladies who had been in the shelter the longest to whom had just arrived. When Honey got to the end of the list, the sip of iced coffee she took, flew from her mouth.

"Whoa!" Lex exclaimed. "You okay?"

Coughing, Honey placed her cup down on the desk. "The new resident... you sure this is her last name?"

Grabbing the sheet, Lex looked it over and nodded. "Yeah. That's what she told me it was last night and that's the name on the hotline sheet from when she called."

Honey gulped. There had to be a typo. There was no way Astryd, her best friend, was in a shelter. Specifically, the one she worked at. She wanted to ask why, but the answer was clear as day. Honey thought back to the events of yesterday and remembered she and Astryd's text conversation. In it, she seemed like her normal self. Astryd didn't reply to her last text, but that wasn't anything out of the ordinary. She was known for forgetting to respond to messages. Now, Honey was questioning what normal was. *How did I miss the signs?* Feeling horrible, but not wanting to divulge her current findings, Honey did her best to compose herself.

"Oh okay. I think I must have read it wrong," she fibbed.

Lex gave her a quizzical look but didn't press

the issue. The rumbling of her stomach reminded her that she needed to eat. After giving her an update, Lex grabbed her things to head home. Slumping into the chair, Honey told herself not to shed a tear while on the clock, but she couldn't help it. Astryd was her best friend, her sister, her... a woman who was getting abused and couldn't come to her friend about it.

With the profession she was in, confidentiality wasn't something the agency took lightly. Honey had been working at the shelter for years, and her friends knew that, but the details of it weren't known. Many days when she left work, she'd vent to Astryd, but never did she imagine coming in and Astryd being the one venting to her. As tears rolled down her cheek, she quickly wiped them when a knock came to the closed office door.

"Come in," she called out.

Peeking her head inside the doorway, Astryd did a double take and hurriedly shut the door. Rushing from her seat and from behind the desk, Honey pulled the door open. With pleading eyes, trembling lips and arms outstretched, she motioned for Astryd to come to her.

"I-I didn't know you worked at this one. I mean, I wasn't even thinking about that when I called. I was just trying to get away," Astryd choked out in a rushed manner.

"It's okay, it's okay. Come in the office."

When the door closed behind them, the two hugged and cried hard on each other's shoulders. Astryd for more than one reason and Honey because she felt her friends' pain. It was bouncing off her so strongly and breaking Astryd down. Holding her friend up as she let out blubbering cries from her gut, Honey then knew that whatever she had been going through didn't just begin. The type of breakdown she was experiencing had been bottled up for a while.

Breathing hard, Astryd sniffled and wiped her face as she lifted up. "I'm sorry. I got your shirt all wet."

"Girl forget about this shirt. Here," she said, handing her some tissue.

Grabbing it, Astryd blew her nose and took a seat in front of the desk. "I guess you want an explanation, huh?"

"No. You don't have to give me one, but I do have a question. Where are the girls?"

"In the room sleep. I was coming to see if I could use the phone to call Grammy. I cut mine off."

"That's why you didn't text me back. Are you hurt? Did he hit you?" Honey asked, going into protective mode.

Astryd squeezed her eyes shut, exhaled, and peeled them open. "There's just so much you don't know and so much to explain. One day, I'll tell you it all, but not today, okay."

"You don't have to. I'm just glad you're safe."

"Is me being here and knowing you going to be okay?" Astryd asked, and her question felt like a gut punch to Honey's ribs.

Their situation was indeed a conflict of interest and Honey knew she'd be on pins and needles all day with them in the shelter. Even if they tried going about it by pretending like they didn't know one another, the girls would more than likely not let that happen. They loved Honey, and once they saw her face, it'd be a wrap.

Seeing the look on her friend's face, Astryd shook her head. "It's fine. I'll just have to find somewhere else to go. I don't want you getting in trouble."

"I won't, but you don't have to go to another shelter. Stay with me. You know I don't mind," Honey insisted.

"No. I can't. He knows where you live and it's

only a matter of time before he realizes I'm not coming home before he starts harassing y'all. I know he'll start with your place first."

The seriousness in Astryd's voice caused chills to shoot up Honey's spine. "It's that bad, Astryd?"

The only response Astryd could give was a head nod. However bad Honey was thinking it was, she was correct. Telling herself not to cry again, Honey sat down next to Astryd.

"So, what do you want to do? Our main priority is making sure you and the girls are safe."

"I honestly don't know. Like, I don't know what I should do or where I should go. I should've never messed with him. He's a fucking psycho, Honey. I never thought I'd be that girl you know? Especially with the way my mom—"

"Ssshh. We don't have to talk about it. Let me figure something out for you okay? No matter what though, this isn't your fault. None of this. What he did to you is because he lacks in areas of his life that you strive in. You're beautiful, intelligent, a great mother, can cook your ass off, you work hard for your own money, kind-hearted, and you love hard and selflessly, plus so much more."

"I loved him so much, I forgot to love myself."

Her revelation hit Honey like a ton of bricks. Astryd's vulnerability at that moment had Honey ready to send her people to her friend's crib and do Alonzo grimy. When her jaw clenched, Astryd shook her head no already knowing what was on her mind.

"No. Don't do anything. If it were just me in this situation, I would have retaliated a long time ago. I refuse to let my girls grow up without me. They need me."

"Yes, they do. We all need you."

The two hugged again, and the wheels in Honey's head began to spin. She had to get her friend help and quick. Though the shelter was safe, Ashlynn had cried all night, and Ashlee peed the bed. Thankfully, there was more than one bed, but that wasn't like Ashlee. Going through the list of people in her head who could possibly be of some help, a light bulb went off in her head as she snapped her fingers.

"What was that for?" Astryd questioned.

"I have an idea. Just… let me see if it's okay and we'll go from there okay?"

Astryd sighed. She didn't have many options, so she nodded. If anyone was going to look out for her and have her back, Honey did. She had a plan, a farfetched one, but a plan nonetheless. Now, if it fell through, she'd be happy as hell.

"I'm not taking the girls to daycare or to Grammy's today, so we'll just chill out," Astryd told her.

"Okay. After I make a few phone calls, I'll let you know what's up on getting out of here. Did you drive?"

"Yeah. I really didn't want to, but the car is in my name, so he shouldn't be able to call the police or anything, right?"

That idea hadn't crossed her mind until now. Honey shook her head no.

"Nah. It would be a waste of time honestly. Just keep your phone off because you know he's going to call."

Astryd nodded her head and stood up. She had no plans of powering her phone on knowing the crazy things Alonzo had sent.

"I-I've never left him before," she said in a shaky, unbelievable breath.

Honey pulled her into a hug. "Well, there's a first time for everything, right?"

Chapter Six

Happy wasn't quite fitting of a word to describe how D'Haven felt. He had just landed a job with Frito-Lay as a fork-lift driver and started working next week. It started off with good pay, and though he was used to raking in much more than nineteen dollars an hour, D'Haven wasn't turning the job down. Especially not with the way his pockets were looking.

Thanks to Winston and Tech, he had a crib, a car, and a nice stash, but D'Haven wanted his own bread. He appreciated them looking out, but money didn't last forever. Especially not when he had practically started his life all over. Thanking the Man above for helping him secure the job, D'Haven hopped in his ride and peeled out the parking lot.

As soon as he hopped on the highway heading toward his mama's house, his phone rang. Seeing Honey's name flash across the screen, he answered her call with a grin on his face.

"What's up, cuz."

"Hey, big head. You busy?" Honey asked.

"Nah. I just left my second interview for my job. What's up?"

Honey squealed. "Oh my gosh! Congratulations! You got it, right? I mean you said your job."

Chuckling, D'Haven said, "Yeah. I got it. Thank you. I start next week."

"I'm so proud of you D'Haven. Seriously. Most niggas get out and be complaining or revert to the life that got them locked up. I swear you need to talk to some of these niggas out here. Make them step their game up," Honey fussed.

"Everybody not as ambitious as me, Honey Doo Wop. You know that," he said, reminded her of her nickname.

"I miss when you called me that," she laughed. "Okay. But, to the reason I called. I need a huge, huge favor. And before you say no, just hear me out."

"I was going to. What does this favor consist of?" He asked, switching lanes.

"Well, it involves three girls—"

"A foursome? What hoes you be kicking it with that get down like that?" D'Haven asked amused and halfway interested, making Honey suck her teeth.

"No, it's not a foursome nasty. It's Astryd and her daughters."

A smirk danced in the corner of his mouth hearing her name. They hadn't talked since the night of his party, and that was over two weeks ago. D'Haven had been so focused on getting his life back on track, women, including Astryd, had been placed on the back burner. Now that he was somewhat on track, he figured he'd see what she was up to.

"Yeah? What about them?"

"Actually, can you just come to my house, so I can ask in person. They're here."

"You just got serious as hell. She good? They good?"

D'Haven's tone let Honey know right then he was going to be pissed when he found out why she needed a favor from him. If she knew the history between the two, Honey would know that pissed was putting it lightly for the way D'Haven was about to feel. That was another secret Astryd had yet to reveal, but she would soon enough.

"Um, I'll let you find out for yourself. I'm texting you my address now. I don't live far from your mama. Like fifteen minutes," she told him.

"Aight. I was headed that way anyway, so I'll see you in a little bit."

"Okay."

The entire way there, D'Haven thought of all the things that could be wrong with not only Astryd, but her girls as well. When Honey told Astryd who she was reaching out to, she put up somewhat of a rebuttal, but not much of one. D'Haven was the only person they could think of who wasn't directly connected to Astryd. Plus, Alonzo had never been to his place or knew who he was.

Pulling into Honey's driveway, D'Haven parked and hopped out. Honey opened the door and let him in. After giving him a hug, she walked him to her kitchen area where Astryd was. Ashlynn was taking a nap in the living room while Ashlee played on her tablet.

When D'Haven strolled through the entryway looking like a damn walking orgasm, Astryd swallowed the extra saliva that gathered in seconds. Dressed professionally for his interview, D'Haven was rocking a black button-down shirt tucked into black slacks, and a pair of black dress shoes. Though she tried not to let them, Astryd's eyes fell to the bulge in his pants. It was just... there, unintentionally calling her name. She felt like a slut for thinking such nasty thoughts at a time like this, but hell, the girl was still a woman, and D'Haven looked good as hell. She wanted to call up Deb herself and thank her for birthing such chocolatey goodness.

"What's up, Pebbles?" He said, kissing her cheek. Her entire frame relaxed at the feel of his lips.

She gave him a soft smile. "Hi. You look nice."

"Preciate it. Now, what's going on? You and the girls good?"

He got straight to the point. There was honestly no need to beat around the bush. Releasing a deep breath, Astryd looked toward Honey for assistance. With ease, she broke down the severity of Astryd's situation. She left out the gruesome details of her being abused, but D'Haven knew what was up. The whole time she talked, his eyes were trained on Astryd. Her entire demeanor was everything but calm. She was a nervous wreck and hadn't had a good night's sleep in almost a week.

Her eyes were heavy with bags underneath,

short hair a curly mess, and her skin wasn't glowing like it was the first day he saw her. In his brief observation, he knew right then that he was willing to do whatever necessary for her. When Honey was finished, she took a deep breath.

"So, is it okay if she stays with you? I know it's a lot and you just came home, but you're the only option. The safest one anyway."

"Yeah. You ready to go now?" he said with ease making Astryd snap her head in his direction.

"Yes?"

He nodded and walked over to her as tears filled her eyes. "Yes. Is that okay with you?"

"Of course. I just don't want to be a burden to anyone is all. Are you sure?"

"Positive, baby."

Honey scratched her head. "Um, I'm sure I'm missing something here. Right?"

D'Haven chuckled. "Nah nosy. You ain't."

"Astryd…" Honey called out, and Astryd grinned softly.

"We kinda have history together."

"Wow. Okay. That's how y'all do me? When was someone going to tell me this?" she said, faking like she was hurt.

"It wasn't much to tell honestly. It was a small crush, and then he went to jail," Astryd revealed.

"So, you don't love a nigga anymore?" D'Haven said running a hand through her hair. "This cut is sexy on you. Fits your face."

She shuddered under his touch and shook her head. "Please don't do that."

"Do what?"

"Run your hand through my hair like that."

Hearing the seriousness in her voice, D'Haven removed his hand and stuffed it into his pants pocket. "Aight. Anything else I can't touch on you?"

"Whew," Honey breathed out, reminding them they weren't alone. "Maybe this wasn't a bad idea after all. Y'all are well acquainted if you ask me."

The duo chuckled at her silliness, but she had a point. Their chemistry was smooth and never forced. D'Haven paid attention to the small details of what Astryd was saying and what she wasn't. Like now, her eyes were gazing lazily into his but shined a little different at his question. She wanted him to touch her, but not in a sexual way. She wanted him to place his strong hands around her heart and pump warmth and life back into it. She'd openly accept his offer if he were willing.

"You sure you're okay with us staying at your place?" Astryd asked again.

"Pebbles," D'Haven sighed.

"I'm sorry. I just—"

"Don't apologize. I get it. You want to be one hundred percent sure that you are welcome in my home, right?"

She nodded as he held her chin in his hand. "Yes."

"As you should be. Y'all are safe with me, okay? Where y'all stuff at so I can take it to the car."

Nodding her head toward the living room, D'Haven removed himself from her space but not before telling her he'd be back. The reassurance was everything she didn't know she needed to hear. Once he was out of the kitchen, Honey came and stood in front of her with her arms crossed.

"Mhm. You got some explaining to do, missy," she sassed making Astryd giggle. "And look! The nigga even got you smiling. Y'all had sex?" she asked in a whisper.

"Oh my gosh," Astryd laughed. "Will you hush?"

"What!? I'm just saying, friend. I know you, and I know D'Haven. I peeped how he was all on you at his party, but now I see why."

"And, why is that?" Astryd asked, playing into her entertaining conversation.

"You want some of that fresh out a jail dick, don't you?"

The laugh that escaped Astryd's mouth was loud. She couldn't hold it in if she tried.

"You've been hanging around Greigh too much. That's something she'd say."

"It's the truth though. Am I wrong?" She asked, cocking her head to the side.

"Mommy, we're leaving?" Ashlee asked, rushing into the kitchen.

Astryd gave Honey a smirk and hopped down from the bar stool she was sitting at. When D'Haven walked back into the kitchen, he had a look on his face she couldn't quite read.

"Yes, Pumpkin. Let me introduce you to who we'll be staying with."

Facing D'Haven, Ashlee looked up at him with sparkling eyes and a smile. She was so in tune to her tablet, she didn't see him come into the living room and grab their bags, before hauling them to Astryd's car.

"Ashlee, this is D'Haven, D'Haven this is Ashlee. The little one sleep in there is Ashlynn."

Ashlee stuck her hand out. "Hi! I like your name," she said, grinning wide.

D'Haven grinned back and Astryd damn near passed out. The simple gesture of him showing off his pearly whites had her reconsidering her stay with him.

"I like your name too. Is it Pumpkin or Ashlee?" he joked.

"It's both!" she laughed as Astryd shook her head. "Only Mommy can call me Pumpkin, though."

"That's okay. Mommy has her own nickname, too," he said before shooting Astryd a smirk that solidified his nickname for her every time he was in her presence.

Her nipples hardened behind the hoodie she was wearing and was grateful she had slipped it over her tank top right before he arrived. As he and Ashlee went back and forth sharing random conversation, her more so talking about the game on her tablet, Astryd felt a sense of peace come over her. She didn't know how long it would last, but she was going to cherish it for the time being.

After Astryd used the restroom and made Ashlee and Ashlynn go as well, they headed toward her car. They gave Honey hugs and promises to see her later in the week before Astryd thanked her and typed in D'Haven's address into her GPS. Honey had an extra phone line through T-Mobile, and it came in handy. Astryd had a new number for the time being. She had yet to power on her phone, but she was able to contact her job and her Grammy.

She had only been at Honey's for three days, and in the time frame, Alonzo had gone up to her job and visited her grandmother making threats. The only reason he hadn't stopped by Honey's was because he couldn't recall what block she stayed on. But, to keep her out of harm's way, Astryd still felt comfortable heading to D'Haven's instead.

Trailing her car just in case Alonzo got fed up and decided to stake the neighborhood, D'Haven wondered what he had really gotten himself into. Helping Astryd out wasn't the issue he had. Containing the feelings he had for her were. Before he got locked up, their friendship was more than a simple crush as Astryd put it. He had taken her virginity the year before he went to jail so to find out she was in a full-blown relationship and had kids by another nigga sort of bruised his ego.

Most men, the ones he had grown up with, didn't prefer breaking a virgin in. They claimed the girls were too clingy and expected the most out of them. In D'Haven's mind, virgins were perfect. Astryd had chosen him to be the man she gave her pureness to, and he cherished it like a mothafucka. That entire summer, they dated on the low but didn't get serious because Astryd was going away to school that Fall. When she came home for Christmas break, they had a heart to heart and decided to just remain friends. The college life had gotten the best of Astryd.

For a few weeks, they kept in contact, but it became less and less. When she popped up with a boyfriend, D'Haven was confused. He thought they had something special but chucked it up as a loss. Three months later, he took the charge for Winston, and they hadn't really talked since. Yet, here D'Haven was offering up his home as a free man to the girl who had in a way played him. Though it was the past, D'Haven had a few questions of his own he wanted to get off his chest.

Pulling up to his townhome, he told Astryd to go ahead and park in the garage. Pulling behind her, he cut the car off and helped her bring she and the girls' things inside. When you first walked in, there was the living room, his bedroom with a bathroom inside, and a half bath for guests. Upstairs was the second bedroom and full bathroom. He told Astryd she and her girls they could have his bedroom for the night since there wasn't a bed in the upstairs room yet.

"You sure?" Astryd asked as the girls made themselves busy scoping the new place out.

"Positive. I can crash on the couch, and we'll go get a bed for y'all tomorrow."

What he really wanted to tell her was that she could sleep in the bed with him, and he'd get the girls their own bed but chilled. She was already trying to get out of one complicated situation, there was no need to begin another.

"Okay, well thank you again. I know this isn't ideal for you. I guess I should've asked if you had a female friend or anything that comes by," Astryd said with a giggle.

"Nah. Honestly, you're the first female I've brought here."

Astryd looked shocked. "Really?"

"Yeah. Why you looking like you're shocked."

"I am that's why. You're fresh out of jail and... I don't know," she shrugged. "I guess I thought you'd be humping on everything moving."

D'Haven chuckled and shook his head. "The only person I've humped on is you at my party."

Astryd rolled her eyes. "Whatever. Can I have

some towels, so I can get them in the tub? Otherwise, they'll be running around here all night."

"Yeah. There should be some in the linen closet inside the bathroom. I'ma order some Imo's pizza. What kind they like?"

"Pepperoni."

"Aight. I'll be in the living room if you need anything."

The look Astryd gave him made him not make a move toward the door. "What?" he questioned.

"Why didn't you ask me what kind of pizza I liked?"

D'Haven smirked. "Because I already know what kind you like. Barbecue chicken, right?"

The blush on Astryd's face was one he could get used to seeing on a regular basis again. "Right. Thank you."

"It ain't nothing."

Walking out of the room, D'Haven's phone rang and Astryd couldn't help but think that it was a woman calling him. Why she was concerned and felt some type of way, she didn't know. He wasn't her man, but the act of him opening up his home to her was a privilege she found herself not wanting anyone else to have.

"I'm tripping," she said aloud. "Come on girls. Let's go take a bath."

"Aww Mommy," Ashlee whined.

"Aww Mommy nothing. You have marker all over you, and so does your sister. Let's go, Pumpkin."

After their bath, too much pizza and watching the Trolls movie on Netflix, Ashlee and Ashlynn were out cold. Astryd placed them in the center of the king-sized bed knowing by the time she came to lie down; their little bodies would be all over the place. Letting out a yawn, she curled up on the couch making D'Haven look up from his phone.

"If you sleepy, you can go to bed," he offered. "I know you probably had a long day."

"I'm fine. I'm just relaxing."

He gave her a nod and hit play on the movie 211. Astryd loved action movies; always had. Twenty minutes into it, her gaze fell back on D'Haven. He was out of his dress shirt and pants and was wearing some basketball shorts with a gray tank top. Astryd let her eyes trail from his covered feet, up his hairy legs, to his defined chest, broad shoulders, and heavily sculpted arms. The veins in them were enticingly sexy. When he popped his knuckles, Astryd imagined his hands roaming her body as he delivered a massage she would gladly pay for. When she squirmed in her seated position, D'Haven looked her way, and she quickly looked at the TV.

Chuckling he said, "Pebbles, you staring at me?"

"What? No," she laughed nervously.

"Come here," he called out, and Astryd froze.

She blinked a few times and mumbled, "Huh?"

D'Haven scratched his jaw and licked his lips. "Come here, baby."

Hesitantly, Astryd stood to her feet and moseyed over to him. It was something about the way he had called her baby, not once but twice today, that had her heart beating uncontrollably. Standing in front of him, she tugged on the pair of shorts she was wearing as he looked up at her with a grin.

"You so fine, you know that?"

"Stop," she whined, shaking her head.

Leaning up, he grabbed Astryd around her waist and sat back on the couch. She was straddling his lap with her arms crossed over her chest. The perk in having small boobs awarded her the luxury in not having to wear a bra all the time, but the disadvantage was her nipples always made a grand appearance. Especially now with their closeness.

"Stop what? You are fine. I make you nervous still, huh?"

"A little. I just… I don't know. We haven't seen one another in so long, and this is the way we reconnect," she sighed shaking her head.

"Would you like that we never spoke again?"

"What! No. Those years without you were hell," she said and D'Haven's brow lifted.

"Yeah?"

Her truth surprised them both. "Honestly, yes. We had a special bond. At least I thought we did."

"I should be asking you that? You went and got a man on me and all," he said, and Astryd rolled her eyes.

"He's far from a man, trust me. I don't want to talk about that, though."

"I don't want to talk about that either."

Astryd's brows furrowed with curiosity. "What do you want to talk about then?"

"Me eating your pussy."

"D'Haven," she groaned, shaking her head as he began to massage her ass cheeks.

"What?"

"That's not the type of talking we need to be doing."

"Why not?" he asked, with a smile in his voice.

When his hands crept up her back, she shivered and inhaled a sharp breath. Closing her eyes, she savored the feel of his calloused hands against her skin.

"Look at me," he called out gently.

She peeled her eyes open. The look in his eyes scared Astryd. They oozed with love, but she wished they didn't. She was scared to love again... scared to love him again.

"I'm not here to hurt you," he said softly as tears gathered in her eyes. "I just want to love you."

"I-I know," she choked out. "I just... please bear with me, okay? I'm not used to being loved properly."

Pulling her closer to him, D'Haven stroked her back and whispered in her ear, "Allow a real man to love you, Pebbles. Can I do that?"

She nodded as a warm tear slid down her cheek. His question saddened her to her core. He never demanded anything of her; always asked permission. It was something she was no longer fond of. Alonzo never asked, just requested. He forced her to do things she'd never in life think she would. He forced her to love his malicious, disgusting ways and stay by his side when really, she wanted to leave him.

"You deserve to be loved, Astryd. All of you."

"I can't be loved," she cried, covering her face with her hands. "Why would anyone want to love me after what I've been through?"

"Because," D'Haven stated gently pulling on her wrists, "You'll learn to love yourself first, and that'll be better than any love a man can give."

She sniffled. "Even yours?"

"Even mine. The type that comes from right here," he said placing a hand over her chest where her heart was beating wildly.

His words were sweet, and Astryd appreciated it them, but she wanted to feel them. She wanted this love D'Haven spoke so highly off to water her insecurities and replenish her dry valley.

"I need it to come from you. Please," she whispered against his lips before placing a soft kiss against them.

Indulging in her advances, D'Haven deepened their kiss and pulled her body flush against his. As his hands trailed her body, Astryd's arms wrapped around his neck. His member thickened underneath his polyester shorts. Her soft groans had him ready to make love to her and even if temporary, give her deep strokes to erase her pain. For now, he'd save the strokes and provide her with something that'd settle her needs and his.

Standing to his feet, D'Haven laid her across the long part of his sectional couch. Astryd stared up at him breathlessly awaiting his next move. Removing her shirt from her body, D'Haven discarded her shorts and lace boy shorts next. Rubbing his hands up her thick, copper thighs, kisses replaced their warmth. Spreading her legs at the knees, D'Haven positioned himself over her body and covered every inch with his lips. Licking here and kissing there, the taste of her made him a feign immediately.

Astryd's body was a masterpiece. He'd gladly love to shoot her in the nude and hang her up on his wall if he was given the opportunity. The TV's light illuminated her skin, showcasing her tiger stripes on her hips, ass, and stomach. There was a light bruise covering her side, and she tensed up when he kissed it.

"You're so beautiful, ma," he said, making his way up to his favorite feature on her body besides her smile.

Taking a nipple into his mouth, D'Haven sucked hungrily and caressed the other breast. Her soft moan made him go harder.

"Ahhh, yes," she whimpered.

Astryd closed her eyes bracing herself for the pleasure she knew would come next as he made his way down her body. It had been years since their last sexual encounter, but D'Haven had memorized her body as if it was his own. With need, he spread her legs more and dragged his palm against her womanhood. It was still fat like he liked it, with minimal hair and coated with slickness. His mouth watered at her aroma. Astryd's bottom wiggled in anticipation.

Flattening his tongue, D'Haven initiated the throaty groan that fell from her lips. Skillfully, he slurped, licked, and penetrated her gushy walls. Astryd was sure to give him a cavity. She tasted so good, D'Haven promised to never purchase another piece of candy again. She was his sweet treat. Thrusting her hips upward, Astryd's hands caressed his scalp as he buried his face deeper. Flicking the tip of his tongue against her clit, Astryd's stomach caved.

"Oh, shit!"

"Sssh, baby," he muffled out.

Before her hearing left her temporarily, that word baby caused her to cream upon falling from his glossed lips. D'Haven was eating her pussy so meticulously Astryd wanted to cry. In fact, a few tears did roll down the sides of her face and pool in her ears when D'Haven placed two of his long fingers inside her warmth and zoned in on her clit like it was the last meal he'd ever taste. Astryd's frame trembled, and he held her down, so she wouldn't flip off the couch.

He wanted every drop of her. Her moans encouraged him to keep going. In a swift motion, Astryd's body was flipped over, ass tooted in the air, and D'Haven's tongue was back assaulting her pussy. Spreading her ass cheeks, he showed it love before venturing back down and wrapping his juicy lips around her fat ones.

"Ooooh, D'Haven!" she moaned softly. "I'm-I'm cumming."

"Cum for me, Pebbles."

Juices ran down her thighs as he brought her to her peak in under a minute flat. When he smacked her ass, Astryd squirted all over his brand-new couch.

"I-I can't take anymore," she huffed, falling flat on her stomach.

Chuckling, D'Haven leaned over her spent body and kissed her pouty lips. Hungrily, she accepted them and licked off her juices. While she sucked on his tongue, D'Haven massaged her bare cheeks with his hands, loving how they jiggled with ease.

"You taste so damn good," he groaned in a raspy manner in her ear before lifting up.

Unable to move, D'Haven left her there to bask in her orgasm while he went to get a warm towel. Turning her over, he wiped her down and kissed her puffy lips while fighting the urge to eat her ass up all over again. Sliding her panties up her legs first, then her shorts and shirt following, he pulled her into his arms and kissed her forehead.

"You feel better now?"

She nodded, searching for her voice. "Yes," she answered softly. "Thank you… for everything."

Snuggling closer into his chest, Astryd sighed. Her eyes were heavy with what she knew would be the best sleep she had in months. Her body was aching in a good way, and he hadn't even blessed her with the dick. He didn't have to; not yet at least. D'Haven meant it when he said he wanted her to love herself first. Sex was good, but it wasn't a cure for healing the broken. It was a temporary fix that he was glad to give her, but he knew this was only the beginning of her healing journey.

Chapter Seven

Frustrated with life in general, Astryd roughly drummed her finger over the scroll wheel on D'Haven's mouse. She hadn't had to look for a place to live in so long, she forgot how tedious the task was. A little over a month had gone by since she'd temporarily moved in with D'Haven and though she was enjoying it, Astryd knew she couldn't stay there forever. Especially not when she didn't have an income to bring to the table.

Astryd had to quit her job, though she had planned to anyway because Alonzo had even gone as far as harassing and harming one of her co-workers. She received word through her boss and apologized immensely, but no words could make up for his actions. Relief came over her when she learned charges had been filed and he had been arrested. She wasn't sure for how long, but him being behind bars was better than roaming the streets.

Before his decision to wreak havoc on the people close to her lives, Alonzo had sent her so many messages on Facebook, Astryd lost count. Having not logged in for a while, Astryd decided to one day last week from D'Haven's laptop and regretted doing so. She had over two hundred message notifications. They were filled with threats, apologizes, GIFs of flowers, tons of the sad face emoji before the anger took over again. She didn't bother to listen to the voice messages he left. Hearing his voice would haunt her in her sleep. The peaceful sleep she was finally able to enjoy without fear.

When her phone rang, she happily picked it up needing a break from her search. Smiling, she answered D'Haven's call.

"Hey."

"What's up? What you doing?"

"Was looking for apartments, but I'm tired now," she giggled. "How was work?"

"Long as fuck, but I don't have a reason to

complain. I'm on my way home. You and the girls ate?"

Astryd's heart swelled at his attentiveness. Since day one under his roof, he had been nothing short of amazing. Every need they had, he did his best to accommodate them. Beds had been situated upstairs for the girls, and though she put up a fight not to, Astryd took his room downstairs. D'Haven would sleep in the bed with her at night but would be up and on the couch by the time the girls woke up. They'd joke about him sneaking into her room like some teenager, but he didn't mind.

They'd finally had sex a few weeks ago, and their connection only grew stronger. D'Haven didn't pressure her at all for it. Seeing her walk around his crib, cook at his stove, leave her scent in his sheets and everything else she innocently did to make him fall in love with her, had him ready to blow her back out during every second she was in his presence. He let her open up to him on her own, though. It gave her a piece of herself back. Alonzo no longer had the ownership he claimed to have over her body. For his patience, though he didn't mind waiting, Astryd put it on him so good, D'Haven was rushing home from work every day and had called in sick once already to dig in her guts and just spend time with her.

"Yes, I cooked, but the girls are still with Grammy. Are you going to the gym?"

"Bet, and nah. I'ma head there. I been missing you all day," he admitted, and Astryd grinned.

"Awww. I miss you too. Are you just saying that beca—"

The loud sound of the doorbell ringing startled Astryd, causing her question to be cut short.

"You have someone coming over here?" she asked in a shaky voice.

Fear crept up on her out of nowhere and crippled her immediately. For as long as she had been crashing at his place, no one had stopped by to visit. Not without her expecting them at least. D'Haven didn't mind having company, but Astryd's safety was top priority.

"No. I'll be there in less than five minutes though. Can you peek out the blinds and see who it is?"

"Um, okay. Hold on."

Standing on trembling legs, Astryd's heartbeat tripled in speed the closer she got to the door. She didn't want to peek out the window, so instead, she looked through the peephole. Relief came over her when she realized it was only Demi; D'Haven's sister.

"It's just your sister," she breathed out.

"I told her about popping up over my shit. You can open the door if you want to, baby. If not, tell her I'm down the street."

Astryd shook her head and began to turn the locks on the door. This was his home, not hers, and she'd never make his company wait on the porch.

"It's okay. I'll let her in," she replied, pulling the door open.

Stunned to see a woman, let alone Astryd, opening her brother's door, Demi stood with a shocked expression on her face. "Oh, wow. Hey. I didn't know you were here. Is my brother here?"

"He's um, on his way. You wanna come in?" Astryd asked as the passenger door to Demi's Impala opened.

"No, I was just coming to drop this money off."

Astryd smiled softly and took the money from her outstretched hand. When she looked up, her smile dropped from her face. She could have pissed her pants had she not gone to the restroom minutes before D'Haven called her. Her eyes bulged, and chest tightened as fear ripped through her chest. She was panicking at the sight of Alonzo leaning against Demi's passenger door. The wicked grin on his face scared Astryd shitless.

"A, what's good baby? You ready to come home to Daddy?"

The sound of his voice confirmed that she wasn't dreaming. He was there in the flesh and Astryd couldn't move. She couldn't believe he had found her and was here with... Demi. Realizing that, Astryd snapped out of her trance just as D'Haven's truck speedily pulled up on the street.

"W-Why did you bring him here?" Astryd asked as her voice cracked.

"Demi!" D'Haven yelled out. Rushing up his driveway, he didn't even glance Alonzo's way. His only concern was Astryd. Seeing the look on her face, he glanced back at Alonzo, and his jaw clenched.

"Pebbles, go inside," he told her sternly.

"Bring your ass here Astryd!" Alonzo belted out.

"Why you got this nigga at my crib?" D'Haven spat his sister's way.

"I-I, we talk," she stuttered causing Astryd's eyes to stretch wide.

"What?"

And, then it hit her. The flowery smell of perfume she had smelled for months on Alonzo's clothing was Demi's. He was cheating on her with this young ass girl, and Astryd couldn't believe it. Demi had not a clue of what monster she was "talking" to, but she was going to find out.

"Y'all talk?" D'Haven scoffed. "He's a grown ass man!" He growled before walking up on Alonzo. "Aye! You need to get the fuck up off my property, homeboy."

Alonzo pushed himself up from the door. "Yeah? I ain't leaving unless my bitch comes with me."

Hearing him call Astryd out of her name, D'Haven didn't even think once before his fist flew into Alonzo's jaw. Having more strength and fueled by anger, Alonzo's weak punches, light ones compared to the ones he delivered to Astryd's body, were no match for D'Haven's.

"D'Haven, please!" Astryd yelled out frantically.

"Bitch ass nigga," D'Haven hissed sending a vicious blow across his head with the butt of a gun.

Astryd didn't know where the gun had come from, nor when he had pulled it out, but she knew he was on probation. Having a weapon on him was the quickest way to send him back to jail. But, something inside him told him it'd be needed. As unlawful as he knew it was, especially in his condition, D'Haven kept one tucked in a compartment in his truck. He had moved recklessly before getting locked up and though he had changed since, the streets hadn't. They were only grimier than before, and niggas were ready and willing to take lives for no reason. In his case, he wanted to dead Alonzo right now; fuck the consequences.

"D'Haven, they're going to call the cops!" Astryd cried out from the porch.

That snapped him out of his daze. Huffing, he stood upright and brushed his nose before tucking his gun in the waist of his jeans. When Alonzo glanced his way and grinned, D'Haven sent a kick to his face that cracked his jaw on contact.

"Oh my gosh," Demi cried. "Stop it!"

He could have broken his neck by how quickly he glanced back at his sister. "You ain't talking to this nigga anymore, so you might as well go in the house. Astryd, go inside, baby."

"Yes, I am! You can't tell me what to do because you're fucking his baby mama. They're not even together!" Demi screamed, foolishly.

"So, you know who he is and still gon' mess with him?" D'Haven asked in disbelief as Demi struggled to help Alonzo to his feet.

"I love him! How could you do this to him for no reason!"

No matter how many times D'Haven told Astryd to go inside, she couldn't. Every emotion known to man filled her body as she watched the man she used to love with every fiber of her being be assisted by his mistress. A girl who had been around Astryd plenty to know that Alonzo was her man. No, Astryd didn't come around much since D'Haven went to jail, but she was around enough.

The look Alonzo gave Astryd as he stood straight up holding his mouth would forever be embedded in her mind. When his eyes left hers and focused on D'Haven, he gave him a head nod.

"H-How could they do this to me?" Astryd questioned painfully. "How could you do this to me!"

Her scream echoed loudly as Demi helped Alonzo in her passenger seat. D'Haven looked her way and frowned, and it deepened with her next set of words. They damn near ripped his heart in half.

"I loved you! I gave you all of me, and this is how you repay me!"

Astryd seemed to want answers to questions he was never going to reply to.

"The fuck you doing all this for?" D'Haven asked her.

"Your sister has been messing with him all this time!" she screamed, ignoring his question.

He sucked his teeth. "Go in the house so we can talk."

"Yeah! Go in the house so y'all can talk. I'm sure you'd love to know that he has a baby on the way, too. Yep. Baylei called me today. Is that what that money is for, an abortion?" Demi spat, before she hopped in the driver's seat and backed out of the driveway so hastily, she almost rammed into D'Haven's truck.

The air became eerily thick with silence as Astryd stared D'Haven down. She was searching for his face for any signs of a lie. Demi had to be lying and just saying that out of anger. She just knew she was. When D'Haven's head dropped, her stomach sank, and heart fell to her feet. Her throat clogged with an unexplainable pain as she tried to get out of his eyesight. The mere sight of him was almost worse than seeing Alonzo.

"A-A baby?" she choked out, blinking with bafflement in her eyes.

D'Haven ran a hand through his short, curly

mane. Guilt consumed him immediately. "I don't know if it's mine for sure."

"T-That's where you went that night," she whispered in agony.

When he didn't answer right away, her tears streamed down her face. The first week at his home, Astryd had a breakdown. She was on the phone crying to Honey over Alonzo's actions. Though he should've been the last person to shed tears over, Astryd was just having one of those days. It hadn't happened since, but D'Haven heard it. He didn't know whether to take it as her missing him or what, but before she could give an explanation, D'Haven was out the door. He headed to Baylei's crib and didn't walk back through his door until six that morning.

Astryd was asleep in his bed, and when he climbed in behind her after showering, he kissed her damp cheek and softly apologized in her ear. Astryd had long ago learned not to question Alonzo's actions, so the following morning, D'Haven's whereabouts the night before was never brought up. Now, she wished she would've said something.

Back peddling into the house, she shook her head as tears ran down her face. She couldn't believe him. After everything she told him Alonzo put her through, he was turning out to be the exact same. No, Alonzo didn't have a baby on her, that she knew of, but damn. The agony felt the same as when Alonzo caused it. Rushing after her, D'Haven tried pleading his case.

"Pebbles, please. Just hear me out."

"No, D'Haven. You know what?" she cried, staring him in the eyes. "I can't be mad at anyone but myself. I should've known better."

"Known better about what? I promise it was a one-time thing. You were crying over that nigga and I just… that shit ran me hot."

"I wasn't crying over him! I was crying for my daughters! They ask about him, and I have to make up lies because the man they call Daddy is a fucking abuser. And, here comes another man they loved turning out to be the same way!"

D'Haven's jaw clenched. "I'm nothing like him."

"No? Well, you explain to them why my heart is broken and why we're leaving then," she yelled.

"You don't have to leave. Can we just talk about this? Come on," he said reaching for her hand. "Please, Pebbles."

"No, D'Haven. Don't come near me," she cried, shaking her head in disbelief.

"I'm not about to hurt you. Let's just sit and talk

this out like adults. I don't have a baby on the way, and you can't leave me," he said.

"You don't know that! And, why can't I leave you? I don't have to stay here!"

"Because I love you."

Astryd began to sob as her head shook uncontrollably from side to side. She couldn't handle all of this right now. His admission to loving her should have been music to her ears, but instead, it was a stab to her heart. The knife penetrated her flesh and twisted causing a pain so discomforting, Astryd could hardly breathe. Rushing to her, D'Haven wrapped his arms around her as she broke down. She didn't want to cry into his strong arms and muscular chest, but she was tired. So tired of the men in her life breaking her and then moving along with their lives as if everything was okay. No one was ever there to pick up the pieces; only there to shatter them.

"You don't love me," she cried as he carried her into their room.

Climbing atop the bed with her cradled in his arms, D'Haven held her down as her body quaked. She was trembling with hurt, and he was the cause of it. Wanting to soothe it all, he placed kisses against her wet cheeks, down her neck, and didn't stop until her shirt was lifted over her breast. Lifting up, he slid her shorts down and shushed her cries.

"Sssh, baby. Don't cry. Please forgive me. I love you, Pebbles," he said kissing her lips, before diving head first between her thighs.

Relentlessly, D'Haven ate her out making her body orgasm so quickly, Astryd could hardly catch her breath. Spreading her legs, D'Haven worked quickly to unbuckle his jeans, place the gun on his nightstand, and slide into her oasis. Astryd's eyes opened the minute his massive dick entered her. His girth stretched her center as they stared at one another. The damage he caused was written in her glossy light brown eyes.

Pushing her legs back so they were chest to chest, D'Haven stroked her walls and kissed her lips tenderly. Astryd knew this was wrong. Sex wasn't going to fix the pain, but it hurt so good.

"I love you, Pebbles," he groaned lowly on her ear. "I'm so sorry for hurting you, baby."

Slow, deliberate strokes elicited pleasurable moans from each of them. Easing in and out of her tight, warm, wet walls, D'Haven whispered sweet nothings in her ear. They were going in one ear and right out the other, though. The dick was good, fucking superb, but Astryd couldn't get her heart and body to be on the same page. D'Haven was trying to make love and each time the tip of his dick touched the back of her walls, they coated his pole making it glisten more with each thrust.

"I-I c-can't believe you," she cried, scratching at his clothed back. "You said you'd never hurt me."

"I know, baby. I swear I'm so fucking sorry," he groaned, kissing her tear-stained cheeks.

The harder she cried, the deeper and harder D'Haven stroked. She wanted him to take all her pain away, though he was the cause of it. She tried to pull him in deeper and push him away all at once. He was smothering her with love… a love she didn't want anymore. It hurt. Just when she thought things were looking up, here came life knocking on her door reminding her that it wasn't done beating her down.

Against her will, her muscles tightened around his dick, and a moan escaped her lips. The sounds of their lovemaking echoed throughout the room as he ran his hand through her hair. D'Haven's back stiffened feeling his nut creep up on him. To keep from letting another moan slip from her lips, Astryd bit down on his bottom lip. She was beyond mad at him, but the dick he was delivering had her cumming back to back like crazy.

"Uuhh," D'Haven groaned releasing all the love he wanted Astryd to feel inside her slick walls.

Spent, but not wanting to let her leave him, D'Haven lay atop Astryd and trailed kisses across her neck and held her in his arms. Eyes wide open, Astryd stared at the ceiling as tears stained the sheets underneath her. The moment they shared was over. She knew it would be temporary, but it started to feel like forever, and that's where she knew she messed up. When something began to feel too good, it was either not going to last and end in tragedy or surprise the hell out of her. Their circumstances had done both.

"Astryd," D'Haven called out, sitting up. "I know you're hurt right now, and I can admit that I fucked this thing between us up. My feelings been involved and seeing you hurt over him put me in a place from my past. Like, you were choosing him again, and that was a bad call on my end. I know it may take a while for you to forgive me, but I'm asking that you at least try. I love you too much to let you walk out of my life again."

Astryd blinked twice, still staring at the ceiling.

"Sometimes, the people we love aren't really who they claim to be," she said flatly, crushing

D'Haven's feelings the same way he had done hers. "They're worse."

Squeezing his eyes shut, he shook his head before lifting off her body. If she wanted to leave, D'Haven wasn't going to stop her. She had been held captive in an abusive relationship for so long, he didn't want to inflict more pain on her than she already had to endure.

Finding the strength to leave, again, Astryd pulled herself up from the bed and stood to her feet. She was hurt by his actions but knew if she stayed more hurt than healing would occur. Swallowing the lump in his throat, D'Haven sat at the edge of his bed and watched her pack up a few of her belongings. The girls had been with Lola for a few days, so she didn't bother grabbing any of their things.

"Where you plan on going Pebbles?" he asked sincerely, as she struggled to carry her bag to the garage. "Here, give me that."

"No. I got it. And, I'm not sure I want to tell you right now. Your sister is fucking the man who... you know what?" she chuckled and shook her head. "Never mind."

"Nah. Say what you were going to say. You

think I knew about them messing around?" He frowned.

"Honestly, D'Haven, it doesn't matter at this point. Alonzo now knows where I've been staying, and I don't trust your sister. I'll figure it out; I always do."

He grabbed her hand gently. "But you don't have to figure it out alone. You know I got you, man. Just put the bags down and let's talk it out."

"No. I'm done talking. I'm no longer relying on words from a man. Yes, your actions at a point in time were enough, but not anymore. I have to work on me. I must learn to love me wholly before depending on you or any other man too. Isn't that what you told me on day one?"

Using his words against him, D'Haven couldn't help but realize that over the weeks she had somewhat become dependent on him. The fact that she called herself out on it was growth in his eyes, no matter how small. Deep down he was applauding her but still didn't want her to leave, but Astryd's mind was made up.

"Can you at least let me know if you and the girls are safe?" he asked, pleading damn near.

"Sure."

Following her into the garage like a sad puppy,

D'Haven watched as she tossed the bags in the trunk of her car, climbed in the driver's seat and slammed the door. As the garage door lifted, she stared at him. Her eyes were pleading for a suitable explanation that would change her mind. Something that would tell her she hadn't made a fool of herself again. In what seemed like no time, D'Haven had put a move on her heart that she knew would take a while to shake. Even the girls loved him, and that saddened her the most because they had grown close with him. Astryd couldn't let the what if's hold her back though. Yet again, her life was in danger. Before, she was sure D'Haven could protect her and her heart, but she wasn't so sure now.

As soon as Astryd pulled out of the driveway and the garage door lowered, the waterworks began all over again. Not out of sadness this time, but out of anger. She was angry at her heart for making such a vast decision in loving him again. Slamming his fist into the door, D'Haven jogged back into the living room to retrieve his phone. Baylei's number was the first one he went to dial, and of course, she ignored it. One night of pleasure that wasn't shit compared to the lovemaking he and Astryd shared had ruined their do-over before it could manifest.

Soft sniffles filled Astryd's car as she made her way to Lola's house. Deciding to let her know she was on her way, she gave her a call. Her grandmother saw things getting serious between her and D'Haven and wanted to give her a break for a few days. Thankfully, she had because they didn't need to be present when all that drama unfolded.

"Mommy!" Ashlee squealed answering Lola's phone.

Her saddened expression brightened at the sound of her baby's voice. "Hi, Pumpkin. What're you doing?"

"Playing a game on Grammy's phone. What are you doing?" she asked sweetly.

"You put games on her phone?"

Astryd had to ask because she knew her grandmother sure hadn't done so.

"Yes, hey!" she pouted as Lola grabbed the phone from her hand.

"Child, I done told you about answering my phone. Hello?"

Astryd chuckled. "Hey, Grammy."

"What he done did? I can hear the sadness all in your voice."

Sighing, she shook her head. It was too much to

explain over the phone. "It's not what he did, but me. I'm on my way there... for good."

Lola didn't wait until they were off the line before she sent a prayer up for her grandchild. "Okay. Drive safely. We'll see you when you get here."

Wiping the last tear, she vowed to let seep from her eyes, Astryd exhaled a deep breath. In the midst of adversity, she couldn't be weak. She could be, but that would get her nowhere. For weeks, she found herself slowly bouncing back to that happy place she had ventured from. It was a place of serenity that was so comforting, this space she was in now was disturbing. A soft chuckle escaped her lips realizing how far she had come.

"God has brought me this far, I refuse to go back. I can't," she said aloud. From her mouth to God's ears, her promise was sealed with faith. Astryd was going to mend her wounds; whether she had a man helping her patch them up or not.

Chapter Eight

wo Months Later

PROMISES KEPT, and faith restored, Astryd hadn't returned to that dark place she was in months ago. With a praying grandmother by her side and strong support from her friends, Astryd was slowly but surely getting back to her old self. A few days after arriving at her grandmother's house, Astryd packed she and the girl's belongings up and headed to a hotel forty minutes outside of St. Louis. She hated the commute she'd make into the city, but it became natural over the weeks.

She hadn't physically heard from D'Haven, but he sent her text messages every other morning. On the days a text wouldn't suffice, he sent her voice messages. Knowing she was over hearing him apologize, he'd ramble on about his workday, what Netflix series he was watching, or what he had cooked for the night. Wanting to feel connected to him from a distance, Astryd would watch the same shows as him, so when he did give her an update, she'd know exactly what he was referring to.

Honestly, she had forgiven him a while ago. It was herself she hadn't forgiven until after getting over his indiscretions. D'Haven was just glad she didn't leave his ass on read and go on about her life. With the bill at the hotel climbing daily, he took it upon himself to send money through Honey or Greigh when they went to visit her. He'd send gifts for the girls and always his love for her through her friends.

Whenever they did come visit, they'd dine out instead of ordering in like they knew Astryd had done all week. Her wounds were still fresh from Alonzo's brutal beating on her mentally, but she found praying and journaling to be the most comforting at her times of weakness. Ashlee and Ashlynn helped as well. They reminded her to live. To keep pushing because she wasn't the only person she needed to survive for; they needed her too.

Things had been going great up until her car stopped working a few days ago. Taking a Lyft everywhere wasn't ideal, considering the cost, but her car wouldn't be fixed for another couple of days. Moving around in another city without fear after being cooped up in her hotel room for weeks, took time but she did it. She had even enrolled the girls in another daycare not far from the hotel. Though she didn't mind them being in her presence, Astryd needed a break sometimes.

Today was one of those days. While the girls were in daycare, Astryd had spent the day pampering herself. She used to love getting her nails done, but Alonzo hated it, so he made her stop. It felt so refreshing to have a fresh gel manicure, pedicure, facial, and wax. Her eyebrows were snatched, hair was freshly blown out and making its way back to its long length. With everything else changing in her life, Astryd decided to try a new color on her hair. The burgundy with copper highlights popped brightly against her fair skin tone and looked gorgeous. Everywhere she went, someone was complimenting her.

Thanking her Lyft driver for the ride, she climbed out the vehicle and strutted to the building that read *Sweet Tooth Bakery*. Having passed by the place more than a few times on their way to the hotel, Astryd decided to stop by and check them out. Plus, it was that time of the month, and she needed something to cure her cravings.

"Hi, welcome to Sweet Tooth. How can I help you?" the cheerful young girls smile was super inviting. There was nothing like excellent customer service.

"Hi. This is my first time here, but I can tell by the smell and looks it won't be my last," Astryd chuckled, eyeing the cupcakes in the display window.

"Trust me. You'll be back. What're you in the mood for?"

Astryd hummed a little before replying, "Definitely something chocolate for myself, strawberry and lemon for my girls. They'd have a fit if they knew I came by without getting them something."

"Okay, so for chocolate lovers, today's special is the double chocolate chip cupcake with whipped buttercream icing. Then, we have regular strawberry and lemon cupcakes. Or, you could do a strawberry cheesecake brownie. Those are our bestsellers."

Everything sounded so good, Astryd decided to get one of each that she recommended. As the girl bagged her treats up, the door chimed as someone walked in. Always alert, Astryd turned to see who was walking in and the heavy lashes that shadowed her cheeks flew up in recognition. *Goddamn.*

That seemed to be her every thought when D'Haven graced the room with his presence. As cliché as it sounded, he was a breath of fresh air, and Astryd was gulping it in. When he hit her with his drool-worthy grin, her eyes sparkled.

"Damn," he said lowly, licking his lips. "You look… stunning baby."

Astryd stood, surprised, and more uncertain than ever on how to reply. Her words were running in circles in her brain unwilling to cooperate to complete a sentence. One that made sense anyway. The vibration in his voice she missed so badly. Hearing it over her speaker was nothing compared to hearing it in person. She merely stood tongue-tied at his examination of her frame.

"What are you doing here?" she finally asked after seconds passed.

"Can I not be here?" D'Haven asked with a chuckle. "This my spot."

Confusion covered her face. "Your spot? You own this?"

"Nah," he grinned. "I mean, I fuck with their

sweets. My mama sent me all the way up here to pick up an order she placed."

"What's the name on the order, sir?" the young girl asked, eager to assist him.

D'Haven had gotten his hair cut low to his head. His goatee was slightly fuller thanks to the winter weather underway, and the black trench coat he was rocking had him looking scrumptious. Astryd was ready to say the hell with her cupcake; he had all the chocolate she needed right there. A nasty thought of her taking his dick to the back of her throat while he stared in her eyes flashed through her mind, and she shook her head.

This is ridiculous. Why does he look so fucking good!

"Can you give us a second," he told the worker while walking up on Astryd. A soft gasp escaped her as his large hands cupped her cheeks. The tenderness in his expression startled and amazed her all at once.

"D'Haven," she called out softly.

"I miss you so fucking much, Pebbles. Goddamn, I've missed you."

The need in his voice softened her heart. She missed him too; more than he could imagine.

"I've missed you too," she admitted.

"Come home, then."

Astryd shook her head from side to side on his palms. "No. My home is here now."

"Bullshit."

Her mouth snapped shut at his bluntness. D'Haven knew her stay here was only temporary. He needed her, had to have her in his presence before he lost his mind. He had been content but now with her in his grasp, inhaling her scent, and feeling her flesh, D'Haven wasn't taking no for an answer.

"Home is where the heart is. That mothafucka is with me," he hissed. "You left it all over my crib, in my car, in my hands, on my dick," he growled in her ear.

Astryd's body shuddered. He was weakening her stance with each word that flowed from his plush lips.

"Please," she begged, desperately needing him to hush. "What about your baby?"

"Ain't no baby."

Those three words were said with finality. Baylei had lied about being pregnant. She was trying anything to get him back, and her attempt in trying to trap him had failed. For weeks, she carried on like a woman with child would, until D'Haven popped up on her ass. He played it cool like he was there to check up on her and of course, she offered him some pussy. Getting her worked up with no plans to blow her back out, D'Haven excused himself to her bathroom. By the time Baylei realized she hadn't dumped her trashcan filled with empty tampon wrappers, it was too late.

D'Haven gave her a sad shake of his head and chuckled before leaving her standing in the middle of her bedroom looking foolish as hell. After that day is when his pursuit of winning Astryd back kicked up a notch. He still wanted to respect her wishes, but there was only so much ignoring a man in love could take. He loved her so much, he'd go back in time and kick his own ass for screwing up what they had.

"Really?" Astryd asked, hopeful, but still having her guard up.

"Really. She lied and had you answered my phone calls, you'd know that."

"I didn't have to answer your phone calls D'Haven," she sighed. "I needed space from you and my chaotic life."

D'Haven pulled her into his embrace as his arms fell around her waist. "And now?"

"And now what?"

"That space... it's ready to be filled again. Come home. I know the girls miss me."

Astryd rolled her eyes, and he softly smacked her ass. "They do. Especially Ashlynn. All she was saying when she didn't see you was 'Where's Haven? Haven coming?'," she chuckled.

"My girls know what's up. On the real though, baby. I apologize for hurting you. I know you need my actions to prove that my words hold weight, and I'm willing to do whatever to prove I'm not the man your heart turned cold against. I love you, Pebbles. You gotta ease up on a nigga and come home. I need you in my world, baby. You and the girls."

When his soft lips pressed against hers, all resolve Astryd had built up crumbled. Their tongues twirled as he hoisted her body against his broad chest. D'Haven was damn near swallowing her lips whole as his hands caressed her body. She had picked up a little weight, but he didn't care about that. When the door chimed, Astryd pulled away, but D'Haven kept her close to him. Pecking her lips again, he rubbed her back to calm her down. She was so worked up, she was sure he could feel the thumping of her clit.

Breathlessly, she giggled and said, "Okay."

"Okay?" He asked for clarification.

Astryd nodded. "Yes, but do you think you can move maybe? I know it's a lot, but I want to be safe."

"We can move across the fucking world as long as you never leave me again," he told her.

"You're on probation," she giggled.

"Aye. I'll break the law for you girl. You better know that."

She did. In a sense, he had done it before and wouldn't hesitate to do it again to ensure her safety. The lengths he was going to go now that she was back in his life would have terrified another man, but not D'Haven. He wasn't confused about what Astryd meant to him, and he would let her know that for as long as he lived and thereafter.

Grinning, Astryd stroked his jawline. "I do. But, before I fully agree you have to buy my goodies."

"The ones in these jeans or...?"

She laughed a good laugh that made D'Haven's heart leap in his chest. He missed that sound so much he didn't realize how soothing it was until she deprived him of it.

"The ones in my jeans can't be bought."

"Damn right. That pussy is priceless," he said nastily in her ear before placing a kiss to the side of her temple.

Leading them over to the counter, his arm stayed wrapped around her waist until it was time to pay for his and her order. Thanking the girl, he grabbed their sweets and took her hand in his.

"Where your car at?" he asked once outside, scanning the small lot.

"In the shop. I took a Lyft here."

D'Haven looked down at her with questioning eyes. "How long it's been in the shop, Astryd?"

She bit down on her bottom lip. "Just a few days. It's no big deal. It feels good to not have to drive."

"That ain't the point. I need you safe, a'ight? No more Lyfts, Ubers, taxis, none of that shit. I'm getting you a rental before the day ends. Where the girls at?"

"Daycare," she answered as he led them to his truck and opened the passenger door. "I was heading to pick them up when I left here."

"Aight. We can go get them and grab y'all's stuff from the room. That's cool with you?"

Still, he was asking for permission. It was the little things like that, that reminded Astryd why she loved him and always had.

"Yes. Their daycare isn't far from here."

D'Haven nodded and pecked her lips, letting

their kiss linger. Rubbing her hands up his hard abs, Astryd sighed and smiled against his lips.

"Keep on," he groaned. "I'ma bend your ass over in this seat and have my way with you."

"Oooh. Out in the open?" she giggled.

"I'ma nasty nigga, Pebbles. Try me."

She shook her head softly and grinned. "We have plenty of time for that. Let's go get my babies and go home."

It was D'Haven's turn to grin. "Yeah. I like the sound of that."

Light conversation on how they'd been filled the car on their ride over. D'Haven let her do most of the talking, loving how she had taken back control of her life. He was raised by a strong woman, so to be madly in love with one was a blessing. When they pulled up to the girl's daycare and parked out front, he didn't even ask if she needed him to come inside. He wanted to surprise them.

"I'll be right out. They're going to lose it when they see you and these cupcakes," she chuckled.

"They fire, too."

That statement made her hustle inside the building. Kids' laughter, cries, and small chatter filled her ears as she stepped up to the desk. She didn't recognize the girl behind it, but her smile was warm.

"Hi. I'm here to get Ashlee and Ashlynn."

"Hello. One second," she said, going through the sign-out list. "Um, Ashlee was checked out, but Ashlynn is here."

Astryd's heart stopped beating, and all the air departed her body. "W-What?"

"Hello. What seems to be the problem?" The older lady Astryd was used to seeing at the desk asked as she approached them.

"She's here to pick up her daughters, but only one is here. Ashlee's dad came to get her. He said she had a doctor's appointment."

Astryd lost her balance and her head began to spin at what just came from the girl's lips. She was trying not to panic and think that the girl was just joking. But, who jokes about something like that?

"No, no, no," she chanted as her head violently shook from side to side.

"Ms. Saxton, I'm so sorry. Was he not supposed to be picking her up?" Glenda asked.

"NO!" Astryd screamed at the top of her lungs.

Hearing the outburst from the car, D'Haven looked up from his phone and quickly hopped when he saw Astryd reach over the counter and grab the girl by her shirt.

"What'd you do!?" she yelled.

"I-I didn't knooow!" the young girl squealed, stricken with fear.

Had she not been flirting with Alonzo and doing her job, she'd know that he was in no shape or form authorized to pick them up from daycare. He wasn't even on the contact list.

"Baby calm down!" D'Haven said sternly, grabbing ahold of her arms.

"H-He took my baby!" she cried into his chest. "He took her, and they let him!"

As he rubbed her back soothingly, his menacing eyes pierced into the young girl's. He knew it was her fault and if something happened to Ashlee, he wanted to remember her face. She was going to pay for her fuck up. Alonzo had been following Astryd for the past week and a half learning her routine. Some days weren't all the same, but he knew once she dropped the girls off, she wouldn't return for a few hours.

Snatching Astryd up was pointless to him. He wanted to do collateral damage. Taking both girls was risky, and the lie he came up with made the most sense. It had taken him far too long to find out where she had been hiding, but finally, Alonzo had tracked her down. She was good at hiding out, but he was a master in seeking revenge. If she thought he'd take her leaving him to the chin, Astryd had apparently forgotten the monster he was.

"I'll alert the police," Glenda stated.

"You do that. If something happens to her, expect this bitch to be shut down," D'Haven spat, fuming inside. He loved Ashlee like she was his own and his body filled with anger seeing how distraught Astryd was.

Before they left out, another worker brought Ashlynn to them, and even her little smile couldn't change the mood. The pout on her face broke Astryd down. Kids knew when something was wrong, no matter how young.

"Haven," she cooed as he lifted her in his arms. "Hi, Haven."

"Hey, pretty girl. Baby let's go to the truck."

Astryd shook her head. "I can't. I can't leave. She'll come back. He has to bring her back," she cried. "You're going to pay for this!"

The young girl backed away from the desk with tears in her eyes. She knew she had lost her job for good. Finally getting Astryd outside, he strapped Ashlynn in her car seat before closing the door. He grabbed Astryd's hands in his and made her lean against the passenger door.

"Calm down, okay? I need you to just relax for a second, so we can think. Where would he take her?"

"I don't know! Oh, my God! Please don't let him hurt my baby."

As she pulled her hands to her face, D'Haven's cell phone vibrated in the pocket of his coat. Reaching inside, he pulled it out and answered Demi's call. She had been off the scene for a little while, but he wasn't going to ignore her.

"Demi, let me hit you back," he answered.

"This ain't Demi, you punk mothafucka."

Alonzo's voice echoed through his cell, and Astryd's head shot up. Placing a finger against her lips, D'Haven shushed her.

"Where my sister at?"

Alonzo chuckled. "Locked away. You see, I hate liars. That sister of yours has been a pain in my ass, but I think we've come to an agreement. Ain't that right Demi?" he called out and laughed sinisterly. "That's right, I forgot. She can't answer because she's a bit tied up right now."

"Listen, you worthless piece of shit. I swear if you—"

"No. That's not how this goes. You listen to me and do as I say, or someone dies. Got it?"

D'Haven's jaw clenched, but he didn't give a reply.

"Good. Now, I need you to bring me my bitch back in exchange for this little girl. I know she's probably standing there with you listening, so she'll love this. I only tolerated her ass because I loved her mama, but I don't want her anymore. She's not mine anyway, so honestly, I could kill her, but I need Astryd in my presence first. Maybe I'll make her watch since she can't seem to leave you the fuck alone."

The words he spoke looped swiftly in D'Haven's brain. Shock and pure hurt resonated on his face before crushing his soul at Alonzo's revelation. If Ashlee wasn't his daughter, he knew she had to be to his. What hurt him most was that he was sure Astryd knew that too.

"Send the address and you better not lay a finger on my child, pussy."

Snatching the tape from Ashlee's face, she yelped, and D'Haven's stomach flipped. Astryd's hands shot over her mouth before she rushed to the front of the truck and threw up.

"MOMMY!" Ashlee screamed.

"Shut up with all that fucking crying!" Alonzo yelled, mushing her in the head with his gun. "Bring my bitch to me safe and sound, and you can have her. I'd say which her I was talking about, but one may not make it."

With that, Alonzo hung up the phone, and a text with an address came through seconds later. Astryd was dry heaving when he approached her side. With tears in her eyes, she looked up at him as she wiped her mouth with the sleeve of her coat.

"She's mine?" he asked plainly.

All she could give him was a slow nod. "I didn't know for sure until you came home. I'm so sorry," she cried.

His nostrils flared as harsh words that would cripple her settled at the tip of his tongue. D'Haven could break her more than she already was right now, but he wasn't going to. Though she didn't do him the justice of hearing him out, he wasn't going to handle this situation the same. Once Ashlee was safe in their care, he'd get the answers he needed.

"Let's go," he growled, opening her door like a gentleman though the felt like being everything but. "For your sake, you better pray he doesn't touch my baby."

When he slammed the door, Astryd's entire

body jumped. She had fucked up, and she knew it. Her day had gone from sugar to shit in a rapid speed. Never did she think Alonzo would go to such extremes like kidnapping, but she should've known better. An abuser will hurt any and everyone associated with their lover if they couldn't inflict pain on them. Alonzo figured since she didn't get the memo, he needed to make an example out of her... for good.

"WE SHOULD CALL THE POLICE," Astryd suggested as they pulled up to the location Alonzo had sent.

Not wanting to put Ashlynn in harm's way, D'Haven had Honey meet them at a market nearby so she could keep an eye on her. His jaw clenched at the sound of her soft, aching voice.

"No. We go in here, and we handle things my way. You've done shit your way for a long time now, and that ends today," he spoke evenly, shutting Astryd right up.

The house he pulled up to was in an average neighborhood that had families living in the homes, kids out in the yard playing with their coats on, and dogs barking in the distance. Alonzo had been using the house for the past week and a half thanks to this chick he messed around with. She was out of town visiting her family without a clue of what was transpiring in her home.

Demi had been there the entire week, tied up in the basement in one of the rooms with no food, drink, or cover. She had the worst cold ever, and her hunger pains were out of this world. Occasionally, Alonzo would give her a sip of water, but it'd only happen on his time. Beating her for not telling him she knew where Astryd was staying happened the same day they pulled up over D'Haven's house. He had manipulated and convinced her that she was the reason Astryd had left him. Demi apologized and sank further into denial and his conniving ways. Before she knew it, weeks had gone by, and she hadn't seen any of her family.

She began making up excuses and ignoring people's calls. When the phone calls got out of control, Alonzo broke her phone, laptop, and cuffed her to the bed for thinking she was going to leave him. That was only the beginning stages, and he had placed a type of fear in her he wasn't able to do with Astryd. Demi obeyed his every word, and he needed Astryd to be on the same page. Since she wasn't, Demi felt his wrath.

Walking up to the house, D'Haven opened the door and stepped inside. The TV in the living room was on with the volume up loud as if someone were home watching it. Piles of dirty dishes were spotted in the sink as they cautiously made their way through the home. Every other part of the home was quiet. When Astryd stepped on a section of the floor causing it to creak loudly, déjà vu settled in. Flashbacks of the dream she remembered having after leaving Alonzo played in her mind. In the dream, she had gotten shot, but it wasn't playing out how she dreamt it.

"We're down here!" Alonzo called out, causing goosebumps to coat her skin.

Hearing his voice come from a door nearby, D'Haven opened it and saw it led to a set of stairs. Grabbing Astryd's hand, he led her down on trembling legs until they reached the bottom. The potent smell of urine, fecal matter, puke and another smell she didn't want to sniff out invaded their nostrils. Tears sprang from her eyes when she saw Ashlee sitting tied up to a chair in the middle of the floor.

"Baby," she cried out, rushing to her but was

pulled back by D'Haven when Alonzo pointed a gun at her head.

"Not so fast, bitch," he spat. "You don't get to call the shots down here; I do."

D'Haven was itching to beat his ass something serious. No, he wanted to kill Alonzo and go to jail for some serious time this go around. He'd gladly take the charge if it meant taking his life and safely securing Astryd's, the girls, Demi's and any other woman he'd bring harm. The fear dancing in Ashlee's eyes tugged at his heart, but he couldn't clam up right now. She needed him.

"We're here, so go ahead and let them loose," D'Haven insisted.

"You really thought we were over?" Alonzo asked Astryd, ignoring D'Haven completely.

Astryd couldn't breathe. This was something out of a gory Lifetime movie that had her holding her breath in every scene. When Ashlee wiggled in the hard chair, Astryd sucked up her fear and responded.

"We don't have to be," she said, and Alonzo's eyes lit up.

"See, that's the shit I like to hear. You miss me?"

Astryd nodded. "Yes. So much, baby. I don't know why I left."

The words leaving her mouth made her cringe on the inside, but she kept a neutral expression on her face. Alonzo smiled a wicked smile and licked his lips.

"What else?"

"D'Haven will never be the man for me. We can start over fresh Lonzo. Just me and you. No kids, no distractions, just me and you babe."

"I never really cared for these kids anyway," he chuckled, looking down at Ashlee.

Now seeing her and D'Haven together for the first time, anger consumed Alonzo. Roughly snatching her up by the arm, he forgot the ropes were on there and damn near pulled her arm out of its socket. Ashlee cried at the excruciating pain and D'Haven's trigger finger itched. After the incident at his home, he had Tech get rid of his gun, but he wished he had it on him now.

"Where's the other one?" Alonzo asked, speaking about Ashlynn.

"Where you left here. Are you ready for it to just be me and you, Alonzo? I'm sorry for leaving you. It'll never happen again. Give the kid to him, and I'll be all yours."

"All mine?" he asked, with a smirk. "Stop walking toward me!" he yelled at her, and she immediately stopped moving. "You," he pointed the gun at D'Haven, "Get on your knees and place your hands behind your head."

When D'Haven began to move slowly, Alonzo flicked his safety off and cocked the gun back. He was tired of playing with them.

"Hurry the fuck up!" he belted out.

With his hands behind his head, D'Haven trained his eyes on every move Alonzo made as he lowered himself to the ground. He was waiting for any sign behind the only other door down there to assure him that Demi was alive, but he felt it in his soul she wasn't. When his elbow brushed against Astryd's thigh, she began removing her coat, shifting Alonzo's attention to her instead of D'Haven.

"W-What you doing, ma?" Alonzo said, loving the way her body looked in the nude one piece.

"I'm getting comfortable," Astryd replied tossing her coat on the couch nearby. "Is that okay with you?"

Her smile weakened him a little, but the sound of heavy footsteps made him grimace and the hold he had on Ashlee's armed tightened. Astryd's strip-tease was supposed to be a distraction but didn't work. Honey had alerted the police and drove them to the home but was supposed to wait for a signal. She couldn't wait, though. Nor were the police about to wait for a sign that probably wouldn't come. Backing away from D'Haven and Astryd, he dragged Ashlee with him near the wall.

"Bitch, you tried to set me up!" he hissed, just as policemen stormed down the steps with guns drawn.

"Get on the ground now!" They ordered aggressively, but Alonzo wasn't moved.

"Make me! This bitch set me up! I just wanted her back, and this is how you do me! After I raised this bitch-ass nigga daughter, you go and play me like that!" Alonzo screamed sounding every bit of deranged that he was.

"Let her go!" a cop demanded, spittle flying from his mouth.

"Nah. Fuck that! I'll let her go when my bitch comes to me!"

D'Haven was back on his feet, wanting to desperately make a move, but didn't want Ashlee to get hurt in the process. Had he had a few more seconds, he was going to rush Alonzo, and just face the consequences.

"I'll come to you. J-Just let her go. Please," Astryd said, walking to him.

"Yeah," he smirked. "Walk to Daddy. No. Do it fucking slow. Any quick movements and I'm pulling this mothafucking trigger."

Swallowing hard, Astryd nodded her head and did as she was told. For her kids, she'd give her life. When she was halfway across the room, everyone held their breaths. When she was in arms reach, he pulled her roughly to him with his gun still trained on D'Haven now.

"Let her go!" the cop demanded angrily.

"I'ma let the little bitch go, geez. Relax," he chuckled. "Walk slowly okay?" he told Ashlee as she looked straight ahead.

When he gave her a light shove, Ashlee began to amble across the room. Astryd held her breath as her baby's small feet traveled freakishly slow to the other side of the room. When a smirk crossed Alonzo's face, and the gun went from D'Haven's body to Ashlee's, time stood still.

"I lied."

BOOM!

The single gunshot echoed throughout the basement, as D'Haven flung his body in Ashlee's direction, but it was too late. Gunfire erupted from the cop's weapons as they filled Alonzo's body up with bullet holes.

"Noooo!"

A bone-chilling scream from her gut erupted from Astryd's mouth. Rushing to Ashlee and falling to her knees, Astryd cradled Ashlee's body in her arms, as her baby struggled to keep her small eyes open.

"My baby! My baby! My baby!"

D'Haven couldn't breathe. The blood decorating his baby girl's shirt had him paralyzed with grief.

"Look what you did!" She shouted, cutting her eyes in the direction of Alonzo's lifeless body. "This is all your fault!"

Large teardrops fell from Astryd's eyes as she rocked Ashlee back and forth in her arms. Memories of when she was a premature baby flooded her mind. Her soft smile and sneaky grin that matched D'Haven's she'd never see again. At that moment, Astryd wanted to die. The notion of living for Ashlynn didn't cross her mind. The police could send a bullet straight to her head, ended it all, because she felt dead already anyway.

"It should've been me. It should've been me," she repeated softly, still rocking back and forth.

Tears fell from D'Haven's eyes as the police desperately tried to pull Astryd away from Ashlee.

The sight broke him down. Crippled his entire existence. He was merely a shell of the man he needed to be right now.

"We need to see if she has a pulse," someone called out, but Astryd was deaf to the commands.

As her body was lifted away from her baby, she screamed and kicked, but D'Haven didn't let her go. Holding onto her tightly, he looked on as the paramedics stepped onto the scene. He couldn't help but think that this was his fault. If Astryd hadn't been broken before, she surely was now, and he knew it his heart there was no coming back from this. Not now, not ever.

Epilogue

ix Weeks Later

"I CAN'T DO THIS."

The soft whimpers escaping Astryd had been concealed the entire ride to the gravesite. She was sadder today than she ever remembered being in her life. Her emotions were all over the place, people had been asking her a million and one questions, and the only person she could stomach to be around was D'Haven.

Her hands trembled as she held the bouquet of fresh flowers in her hand. She loved the fresh ones; never fake. Crouching down, Astryd looked over her shoulder at the parked Audi truck. D'Haven was leaning against the driver's door with his hat pulled low over his eyes and hands tucked in the pocket of his trench coat. Sighing, Astryd focused on the tombstone before her.

"Ma, happy birthday," she exhaled. "You would've been forty-seven this year."

She sniffled and released a chuckle. "I know, why am I keep tracking of your age? It's because you looked so good at your age and I just want to be as beautiful as you were."

Her words clogged her throat. Six years ago, when Astryd was eight months pregnant with Ashlee and on bed rest, Sienna was on her way home one night and made a quick run to the store to cure Astryd's crazy cravings, but never returned home. While there, a guy tried getting her number, but she politely declined his advances. When she finished getting their snacks and pumping her gas, he approached her again, but this time without words. When Sienna went to speak, the barrel of a gun was pressed into her stomach before a single bullet entered it.

A complete stranger had ended her life because she didn't want to give him her number and since that day Astryd felt like it was her fault. Had she not been pregnant, her mother wouldn't have been working extra hours late at night, nor would she have been stopping to buy her snacks. Astryd was sick with grief, and guilt for years and still was, amid her grieving, she found comfort in Alonzo's arms.

At the time, his controlling behavior came off as him caring for her but looking back now, Astryd knew they were all red flags. She wondered for years why a man felt the need to just kill a woman because she didn't want him, and she never got an answer. She summed it up as them being utterly sick in the head. Alonzo was the same. He had a thing for control, but it got out of hand and turned into abusive behavior. Astryd wasn't the first woman he abused, but she was the one willing to stay. She and Demi.

Unfortunately, Demi's young life ended before anyone could save her. She and her unborn child was pronounced dead on the scene, and Alonzo had known that before he even made the call from her phone. D'Haven and his entire family were devastated and still were by the news, but they gained an extra family member; Ashlee. It couldn't make up for the pain in their hearts with losing Demi, but it helped some.

"I miss you so much. Grammy and I both miss

you," she sighed. "Thank you for watching over me all these years. You really were my guardian angel."

Astryd let silence surround her as the brutal February wind blew her hair out of her damp face. There was so much she wanted to say, so much she had said, but it hurt her to her core that she couldn't verbalize her love for her mother in person. That privilege was snatched away from her, and the guy responsible was serving life in prison. It's what she wished Alonzo was serving, but the cards for him didn't play out the same.

Walking back over to the truck when she was done, D'Haven greeted her with open arms. Wrapping her arms around his waist, he placed a kiss to her forehead, and they both sighed. He of all people knew how much her mother meant to her and for him to remember after so many years what today was made her love him so much more.

"She'd like her flowers," he said as she gave him a soft smile.

"She would. Thank you. I don't deserve how good you are to me."

D'Haven kissed her quivering lips. "Hush. Yes, you do. If anybody deserves all this good loving, it's you."

"Mommy!" a sweet voice from the back seat called out as the window rolled down. "Can we go now? I'm tired of this cast on my arm."

The couple grinned at one another and shook their heads. Ashlee had been excited for her six-week checkup all week. When Alonzo shot her in the back, the bullet made a clean exit. She was in the hospital for a week but survived. The yellow cast on her arm was caused by him tugging on it. He had broken it and was even worse once she fell to the ground. She passed out from the pain, but she survived and now had a scar on her chest.

Astryd still cried to this day when she saw it or thought about how she'd gotten it. She was grateful for her baby to be alive and was even more thankful that she and D'Haven could discuss her secret. Astryd had a gut feeling that she was D'Haven's, but by that time, Alonzo was in the picture, and he was in jail. The abuse had begun while she was pregnant, but she didn't say anything. Too afraid that he'd do the same thing the guy did to her mother, Astryd stayed, and it only got worse.

Alonzo knew Ashlee wasn't his, but to keep the peace and her in his life, he didn't say anything. Instead, he knocked her up with Ashlynn and made a happy, or not so happy, family. He didn't know who D'Haven was until he called her phone a few times while locked up, but he shut that down. By the time he got out of jail, Alonzo knew he had Astryd so brainwashed, she was never leaving his side, especially not for another man. But, she had. It came with a sacrifice, but in the end, it was all worth it. Their love was worth it.

"Yes, Pumpkin. Just give us a second," Astryd replied and the window lifted.

D'Haven chuckled and rubbed his cold hands underneath her shirt making her squirm. "That's your daughter."

"She's really all you. She just looks like me."

"With your fine ass. You think they need a sibling? I mean, we've been putting in work like a mothafucka," he laughed but was serious.

"I've been putting in work. Ever since I rode your dick on the couch at your old house, you got lazy, but the dick still good," she said playfully rolling her eyes. "Better than good."

D'Haven smacked her plump booty. "See, that's why I love you. You call me out but still give me my props."

"Mhm. I love you too. Always have."

Smooching her lips once more, he held onto her hips as they walked around to the passenger side.

"I hope it's not broken anymore," she said.

"What? Her arm?"

"Yeah. She hates that cast."

He pulled her door open. "She'll be happy that it's healed though. You can't always repair things that break, so she's lucky."

Astryd stared up at him, taking his words in but with a different meaning. D'Haven caught the look in her eyes and hit her with his handsome grin.

"Honestly, I'm the lucky one. I'm not done healing yet, but that's okay. I may have been broken, but I'm not destroyed," she said proudly, and he nodded.

"Not at all, Pebbles. You're the strongest woman I know. Let's see how strong you are when baby girl cries about this cast at her visit," he chuckled before pecking her lips once more and shutting her door.

The smile on Astryd's face had been present more in the last few months than it ever had with Alonzo. She reminded herself and heart daily that being broken wasn't so bad; not when the right kind of love, self-love, could mend it. Astryd had learned to love herself with no help from a man, but D'Haven's was something worth thanking God for.

Finally, she was free. Her chains had been broken, and Astryd could breathe again. This time with a new beginning. One that she'd cherish for the rest of her life.

The End...

Message from BriAnn

First and foremost, I must thank God for allowing me to pen such a heart-riveting tale. As a social worker, I work with women like Astryd every day. I pray for women like Astryd every day. To my readers, new and old, thank you so much for taking a chance on this novel. Your support means everything. If you enjoyed it, please drop me a review and recommend it to someone you think may need to read it. I'll have paperbacks available on my website for the Holiday sale this month as well.

Though fictional, some women and men experience abuse in the form of love every day. Please understand and be aware that domestic violence is real and happening in our society. If you or anyone else would like to seek help, please reach out. The Hotline can be accessed 24/7 through the nationwide number 1-800-799-SAFE (7233). Also, my inbox is always open to chat.

Love always,
Bri!

Also by BriAnn Danae

Stay Connected

Join Going Beyond The Book Reading Group

Facebook LIKE Page

Other Books By Me

Speechless When Love Hurts 1-3

I Was Never Supposed To Love You 1-3

She Used to be The Sweetest Girl

He Want That Old Thang Back 1-2

Juvie & Solai: A Hood Love Story 1-4

Feenin' For A G 1-2

The D-Boy Type Is What She Likes 1-2

Sen & Neicey: Life After Love

A Senful Holiday

My Heart Is A Fool 1-2

My Heart Was A Fool

The Love

Am I Good Enough To Love?

In No Need For Love 1-2

She From The Gutta 1-2 (Yaz & Lucci are getting a book)

Phresh & Nykee: Loving You Past The Pain 1-3

Made in United States
Orlando, FL
06 March 2024